SUPERFAN

For all the Superstars I've loved to watch since I was a kid.
And especially for WWE Hall of Famer "The Unpredictable"
Johnny Rodz, who pumped iron next to me at the Gladiator's
Gym on Manhattan's Lower East Side.

GROSSET & DUNLAP
Published by the Penguin Group
Penguin Group (USA) Inc., 375 Hudson Street,
New York, New York 10014, USA
Penguin Group (Canada), 90 Eglinton Avenue East, Suite 700,
Toronto, Ontario M4P 2Y3, Canada (a division of Pearson Penguin Canada Inc.)
Penguin Books Ltd., 80 Strand, London WC2R 0RL, England
Penguin Group Ireland, 25 St. Stephen's Green, Dublin 2,
Ireland (a division of Penguin Books Ltd.)
Penguin Group (Australia), 250 Camberwell Road, Camberwell,
Victoria 3124, Australia (a division of Pearson Australia Group Pty. Ltd.)
Penguin Books India Pvt. Ltd., 11 Community Centre,
Panchsheel Park, New Delhi—110 017, India
Penguin Group (NZ), 67 Apollo Drive, Rosedale, Auckland 0632,
New Zealand (a division of Pearson New Zealand Ltd.)
Penguin Books (South Africa) (Pty.) Ltd., 24 Sturdee Avenue,
Rosebank, Johannesburg 2196, South Africa

Penguin Books Ltd., Registered Offices: 80 Strand, London WC2R 0RL, England

ISBN 978-0-448-45611-9   10 9 8 7 6 5 4 3 2 1

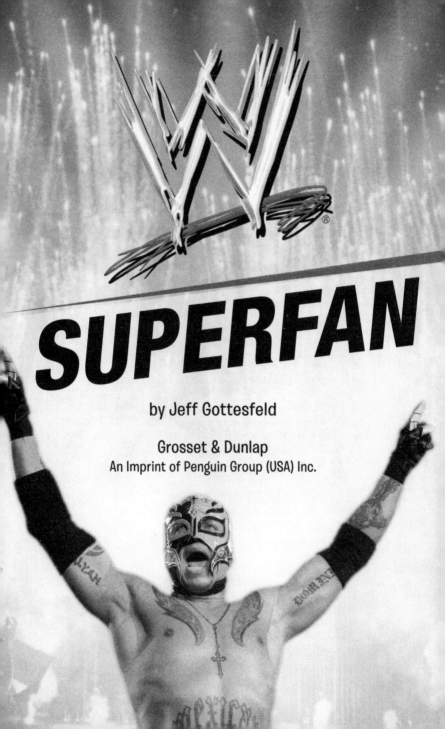

SUPERFAN

by Jeff Gottesfeld

Grosset & Dunlap
An Imprint of Penguin Group (USA) Inc.

CHAPTER ONE

"Oh, say, can you see, by the dawn's early light,
What so proudly we hailed at the
twilight's last gleaming?..."

Shawn Reynolds, part of the huge crowd that filled the Scottrade Center in St. Louis, stood in silence with his father and younger brother as pop singer Sheryl Crow—a St. Louis native—sang the first words of the "Star-Spangled Banner."

Shawn had been doubtful when his brother, Peter, had announced that what he wanted for his tenth birthday was to attend a World Wrestling Entertainment live event in St. Louis. It was a long drive from their home in Columbia, Missouri, to St. Louis, and the night would end late. Their parents were pretty strict about the boys sticking to a regular bedtime. Plus, how could they even get tickets?

"Please, Shawn," Peter had begged. "If I ask Dad, he'll say no. But if we both ask . . ."

It wasn't such a shock that Peter wanted to see the WWE in person. He was a huge fan, as was their dad, Sanford. Shawn, though, had never cared for wrestling. Basically, he thought it was the dumbest thing ever. Still, Shawn had chimed in on his brother's behalf and had even found three tickets on a local website. The kicker was when Shawn donated some of his snow-shoveling money to help pay for the tickets.

Just a week ago, Peter had come out for breakfast to find the tickets on the table. He'd been thrilled. If only they could have found a fourth. Not for his mom, Carla, who would be working that evening—she was a children's librarian at the Columbia Public Library. The fourth ticket would have gone to Alex Garcia, the son of the Reynoldses' closest family friends and one of Shawn's best buddies. Alex was the world's biggest WWE fan—even bigger than Peter.

Shawn glanced to his left. Next to him was his tall, athletic dad, standing ramrod straight like the soldier he was. Beyond his dad was Peter, who had the same short, brown hair and blue eyes as Shawn and was nearly as tall, even though he was two years younger.

As Sheryl soared into the final verse, Shawn wondered how she could sing in front of twenty thousand people. If it were him, he'd have bolted a long time ago since he suffered from body-numbing stage fright. He never played his guitar in front of people. An oral report in school? That gave him actual hives.

". . . o'er the land of the free and the home of the brave!"

The song ended, the crowd roared, and indoor fireworks blasted skyward.

"Whaddya think, Shawnie?" his father boomed, taking in the atmosphere. "You lovin' it?"

"Not sure, Dad," Shawn replied. Every so often, he tried to watch the WWE on television with his father and brother. He never lasted more than one bout.

Sanford laughed heartily as they all sat down. "It's okay to say no, son. I'm a soldier. My commanders specialize in saying no!"

"Well, I'm a fan, Dad," Peter piped up. "When I grow up, I'm going to be the chief executioner of the WWE!"

Shawn smiled. His brother was constantly using big words, and he didn't always use them correctly. Right there, for example, he meant to say "chief executive," meaning "boss," instead of "executioner," meaning "someone who puts another person to death for a crime they committed."

Sanford shook a finger in mock warning. "How about you finish elementary school before you make a career choice."

"Ladies and gentlemen!" A voice boomed over the public address system. "Welcome to a very special winter break edition of *WWE Raw*!"

"Here comes a cameraman!" Sanford pointed to an approaching TV cameraman. "Hold up your signs!"

Shawn and Peter had made poster board signs for the show. Actually, Shawn had made the signs, since he was a good artist and Peter had the talent of a garden slug. Peter's sign featured the WWE logo and read: I LOVE *RAW* AND IT'S MY TENTH BIRTHDAY! Shawn's read: HEY! PUT MY BIRTHDAY BRO ON TV!

To Shawn's surprise, the cameraman stopped in front of them. "Hey, birthday dude and his big bro!" he called in a raspy voice. "You're on television!"

Peter waved his sign wildly. The people in their section cheered.

"Hey, birthday dude!" the cameraman shouted. "Say hey to your mom at home!"

"She's working!" Peter protested.

"Say hey, anyway!"

"Hi, Mom!" Peter yelled, and waved his sign again.

As the cameraman moved on, Shawn felt his cell phone—an older model that used to belong to his dad—vibrate in his pocket. He wondered if it was his mom, somehow watching from the library. "Hello?"

"Hello? Hello? All you can say is *hello*? This is the most amazing thing ever!" It was Alex, and his words tumbled on top of one another. This was typical. Alex either loved something or he hated something. He was never neutral. "I got you and Peter on my DVR! You guys are so lucky! Uh-oh. My mom is yelling at me! Gotta go!"

End of conversation. It was a good thing, though, because at the far end of the arena, a giant video display started flashing multiple colors. Irish rock music blared, and the hugest, palest, most red-haired man Shawn had ever seen strutted through the entrance. "That's Sheamus. He's the number one contender," Sanford explained as the crowd booed. "Everyone hates him."

"He's so pale, he looks like human mayonnaise," Shawn joked.

Sanford cracked up. "That's what Cena always says."

"Who's Cena?"

"John Cena. My favorite wrestler. Look. Sheamus has a mic. Let's listen," Sanford replied.

The lights dimmed, and spotlights glinted off Sheamus's pasty skin.

"Hello, St. Louis!" Sheamus had a serious Irish accent. "I'm not even scheduled to wrestle this evening. I guess the *Raw* general manager didn't want to give you people a display of actual talent!"

The boos grew louder. Shawn heard his dad and Peter join in. He wondered if he should, too. This guy gave new meaning to the word *obnoxious*.

Sheamus wasn't fazed. "That's okay, that's all right. I'll see all these boys—not men, *boys*—in two months in Atlanta at WrestleMania when I take away John Cena's title!"

Shawn didn't know much about the WWE, but he knew about WrestleMania, since his dad ordered the pay-per-view every year. It was the WWE's biggest event. Most WWE shows were held in arenas like this one. But WrestleMania took place in huge football stadiums. Sanford had told Shawn that even when he'd been overseas on active military duty, he'd gather with the guys in his unit to watch WrestleMania on a closed-circuit feed.

The bell sounded to start the night's matches, but Sheamus wasn't done. "I've changed my mind," he bleated. "I think I *will* wrestle tonight. I don't care what the first match is supposed to be. I've been the champion, I'm the number one contender, I'm giving you all a winter break surprise. *Raw* general manager? Make me a match!"

Suddenly, loud music started up—intense hip-hop.

"Whacha gonna do when we come for you?

Booyaka, booyaka, 619! Booyaka, booyaka, 619!"

"Rey Mysterio! That's his theme music!" Peter shouted.

All around Shawn, people were calling the Superstar's name. Shawn expected an oversize athlete like gigantic Sheamus, so it was a shock when a small man ran into the arena in time to the music. He wore loose-fitting red pants and a red, black, and white mask that covered his hair, forehead, nose, and cheeks. He received a thunderous welcome. Shawn glanced at Sheamus. He was twice the size of this little dude.

"Sheamus is going to kill him," Shawn guessed.

"Maybe not," his dad replied. "Rey's fast. Rey's

smart. Rey knows it's not how big you are. It's how you face your fears and overcome them. The match isn't over till the ref counts to three."

The crowd erupted as Rey launched himself into the ring and did a back flip–front flip combination just for fun. Then the bell sounded, and the two Superstars collided.

Sheamus tried to use his superior size to his advantage, while Rey relied on quickness and agility. Sheamus smashed Rey to the canvas with a short-arm clothesline and managed a two-count. A moment later, Sheamus lifted Rey overhead like a baby, spun him around, and then hurled him to the floor outside the ring in a powerbomb. Rey lay on the cold concrete for a count of eight, but somehow got back in the ring.

Sanford leaned toward Shawn. "Look at Sheamus. He can't believe Rey even got up!"

Angry that he hadn't been able to finish off Rey, Sheamus tried to hoist Rey, but Rey slipped away and bounded to the top ropes of the corner. The crowd cheered, which got Sheamus even angrier. "Show me what you've got, little man!" he bellowed.

Sanford leaned over to Shawn. "Last October I saw Rey in this amazing match against Alberto Del

Rio. It was the night that *SmackDown* moved over to the Syfy network," Sanford related as Rey and Sheamus crisscrossed off the ropes. "He pulled that one out. Maybe he can do it again."

"Never heard of Del Rio," Shawn admitted. "The only Superstar I kinda know is Shawn Michaels, and that's because you guys named me for him. You told me he retired."

"Why didn't you name me for a Superstar, too?" Peter asked.

"Because your mom wanted to name you for a saint," Sanford responded.

Peter got the last word in, as usual. "She goofed."

"Come on down, you runt!" Sheamus taunted Rey loudly enough for Shawn to hear.

Rey came on down. He did a flying forward flip and snapped his legs closed around Sheamus's head. Momentum flipped Sheamus. A millisecond later, the Celtic Warrior's shoulders were pinned to the mat.

"One, two, three!" the crowd chanted as the referee slapped the count on the canvas.

The match was over. The arena went crazy.

If a guy like Rey can beat a huge guy like Sheamus, then maybe there's hope for a little guy like me, Shawn

9

thought. So many times in his life, especially on the ball field, he'd been made fun of.

Sheamus bounded to his feet, astonished and angry that he had lost. The audience booed again. Shawn assumed they were booing Sheamus, and Rey must have assumed that, too. Neither saw a heavily tattooed Superstar sneak toward the ring holding a red gym bag.

Peter saw him first. "That's CM Punk," he shouted. "He hates Rey!"

"Rey hates him, too. They've been feuding for years," Sanford explained to Shawn.

The crowd tried to get Rey to pay attention, but he was too distracted by Sheamus. Punk approached Rey unnoticed. Suddenly, Punk swung the gym bag with all his might, catching Rey on his right ankle. Clearly, there was more in the bag than just workout gear, since Rey crumpled, clutching at his ankle.

The crowd screamed at Punk. He smiled and shook hands with Sheamus to even more boos. Then the two Superstars walked together to the exit.

Silence fell over the arena. Rey slowly tried to stand.

As Shawn watched in dismay, Rey fell back onto the canvas, pounding it in frustration.

"That's so wrong!" Shawn exclaimed to his father.

"You care?" Sanford asked.

"Of course I care!"

"If you care, you're on your way to being part of the WWE Universe," Sanford declared.

Right then as he looked worriedly at Rey still sprawled on the ring's canvas, Shawn didn't know if his father was right. What he did know was that he hated CM Punk for what he'd just done to a Superstar who'd done nothing to him.

CHAPTER TWO

Ten minutes later, Rey was helped from the ring.

"He'll find a way to get back at Punk," Sanford told Shawn.

"Not if he can't wrestle!" Shawn shot back.

Sanford pointed. In the ring was a huge, dark-haired man in a suit and tie. "Look. That's Vince McMahon with the microphone. He's the head of the whole WWE. Maybe he'll do something."

Mr. McMahon raised his hand for silence. "What you just witnessed, ladies and gentlemen, was one of the most disgusting acts by a so-called *Superstar* in the storied history of the WWE. CM Punk! You're a punk!"

The crowd roared, then booed as Punk appeared on the huge screen via a feed from the locker room. Shawn wondered what he could possibly say. Would he apologize?

No way.

"Mr. McMahon—Mysterio's been ducking me for months. He deserved it!"

Even Shawn found himself booing until Mr. McMahon quieted the crowd again. "Actually, CM Punk, the joke is on you. Forget WrestleMania. You're not wrestling again until Rey Mysterio says you can. How about that?"

"What?" Punk was livid. "That's not—"

"Bye-bye, Punkie Pie!" Mr. McMahon waved at the irate Punk, and the crowd went wild. Shawn was thrilled. Punk had gotten what he deserved.

Then Mr. McMahon welcomed two more Superstars to the ring.

"The big guy in the purple shirt is John Cena. He holds the WWE Championship," Sanford explained as the crowd roared. "The other guy is Kofi Kingston. He's really fun to watch."

Cena took the mic. "There are a lot of young people here tonight. Hello to the next generation of the WWE Universe!"

Cena handed the mic to Kingston, who swept his hand around. "Parents, thanks for bringing your sons and daughters!"

More cheers. Shawn looked at his brother. Peter was beaming. It made Shawn feel great that he'd helped make this evening happen. He wasn't having such a bad time himself, either.

An aide handed Mr. McMahon the WWE Championship. "This is the WWE Championship," he declared. "Normally, the champ carries this himself. At this WrestleMania, we're doing it differently. It will be carried in by a young person who earns the title of WWE SuperFan. Our first SuperFan will be strong, determined, and dedicated. He—or she!— will represent the young WWE Universe at events in the year to come. He or she will earn a full college scholarship to be placed in a trust until the SuperFan is ready to start school. For more information, visit WWE.com, the official website of the WWE!"

Shawn saw that Peter was so excited about the contest that he was practically climbing on their dad. "Can I enter? Please? I'll be the most soporific SuperFan ever!"

Shawn grinned. He knew that *soporific* meant "causing sleep," not "super-duper," like his brother intended.

"It depends," Sanford said gently.

"On what? It depends on what?"

"It depends on the rules."

Peter thought for a moment. "Yeah. That's right. But if I can, will you let me?"

Sanford gave the all-time parent non-answer

answer. "We'll see." Then he turned to Shawn. "How about you, Shawn? You want to enter?"

Shawn shook his head. "Peter and Alex for sure. But me? Not so much."

Sanford looked disappointed. "You seem to be having fun tonight."

It is true, Shawn thought. *I am having fun. But I am no SuperFan. Not even close.*

"Well, you're allowed to change your mind," Sanford told him.

Shawn nodded. "Got it, Dad."

If Peter or Alex entered, he'd do everything he could to help them. But tonight was a onetime thing. No way was he joining the WWE Universe.

No way.

CHAPTER THREE

The morning after the *Raw* show, Shawn slept until nine. Peter was still asleep when Shawn woke up, got dressed, and quietly left their room.

The Reynolds family lived in a small, white-frame ranch house with just two bedrooms, a living room, dining room, and kitchen. Compared to other kids he knew, the house wasn't much, and Sanford did all the work on it himself. In fact, the day before *Raw*, Shawn had helped his dad repair his bedroom's drop ceiling. Between Carla's librarian job and Sanford's work for the city recreation department, they couldn't exactly afford a contractor.

When he came into the kitchen, Shawn wasn't surprised to see his mom. She had Tuesdays off; it was the day she generally read a few of the new teen books that publishers sent by mail even before the books went on the library shelves. She always said that parents and librarians needed to read everything that their kids were reading.

Today, though, his dad was at the table, too.

Weird. Usually Sanford had to be at work by nine. Was he sick? Shawn's folks were just sitting there, cups of coffee and cell phones in front of them.

Shawn suddenly got a terrible feeling. The last time he'd walked into a scene like this, his grandfather in Chicago had passed away overnight. "Is everything okay?"

His father shifted, his eyes weary. "Everyone's healthy. That's the most important thing."

That was another parent-type non-answer, and Shawn knew it. "Just tell me," Shawn pleaded. "Tell me what happened!"

His father frowned; his mom put a comforting hand on his arm. "Go ahead, Sanford. It's who you are," she told him in the Southern drawl she'd never lost since her childhood in North Carolina.

It's who you are . . .

"Okay, Shawn," his dad agreed. "Then I want you to try to enjoy your vacation." He pointed toward his cell phone. "You know how even though I'm not a full-time soldier anymore, I'm still part of the army?"

Shawn nodded, though he was starting to get a hollow feeling in his stomach. "That's why you train for a weekend every month. It's called the reserve, right?"

"Right," Sanford declared. "We reservists are here if the army needs us." He hesitated. "Well, they decided they needed my unit. We're being deployed. To Afghanistan. I'm sorry."

Deployed? To Afghanistan?

"When do you leave?"

"Friday."

Oh no. Shawn always knew this was possible, but it had never happened before.

"We'll talk more later," Carla told Shawn. "I'm sure you have a lot of questions."

His mother was right. Shawn had plenty of questions. "Will you have to write us letters by hand?"

His dad's laugh was genuine. "It's not like in old movies. I'll be able to e-mail at the base. Maybe even Skype. You'll get so much e-mail you'll be sick of me."

"I think that's unlikely, Sanford," his mother commented dryly as tears welled in her steel-gray eyes.

I can't cry. That's not what Dad needs now, he told himself.

Normally when Shawn was feeling down, he liked to play his guitar. But he didn't want to wake Peter. So he told his folks that he was walking over to Alex's and fled.

Ten minutes later, Shawn was with Alex in the Garcias' lovely family room. Though Alex lived close by, his house was a lot bigger than Shawn's place. Alex's dad ran a printing business while his mom—an amazing cook—did party catering.

The Garcias were upset to learn that Sanford was being deployed. After promising to help Shawn's mom any way that she could, Mrs. Garcia suggested that the best thing for Shawn to do was to keep things as normal as possible for Peter.

"I can help, too!" Alex turned to his mom. "But can we use the computer now? To find out the rules for SuperFan?"

"You haven't looked them up?" Shawn was surprised.

"The Internet's been down since last night! It's the worst! I still can't believe you were there. It was the best *Raw* ever! Rey Mysterio's gonna mess up CM Punk when he comes back. Maybe if I'm the SuperFan, I'll be there for it!" Alex was his usual mass of enthusiasm.

Mrs. Garcia gave Alex permission to log on, so Alex went to the computer while she sat with her laptop on the couch.

"Oh yeah!" Alex exclaimed. "We're back online! Whoa! Check out the WWE website! It's all SuperFan, all the time!"

Shawn peered over Alex's shoulder. Alex wasn't kidding. The WWE home page featured a continuous video replay of Mr. McMahon's big announcement.

"What are the rules?" Shawn asked. "Can Peter enter?"

Alex clicked on a button and shook his head. "Nope. Gotta be between eleven and thirteen."

Shawn frowned. Peter would be bummed. Well, maybe next year.

"There's an online application a parent needs to submit. They want you to upload a video explaining why you should be chosen. They're bringing four finalists to Atlanta for WrestleMania weekend in April." Alex turned to Shawn. "It's a total piece of cake! I should definitely win!"

"Can I see that?" Shawn asked.

"Sure! You aren't thinking about entering, are you?"

Alex got up. Shawn leaned in toward the monitor to check out the rules. You needed to be strong, dedicated, and a person who cared about your community. If you were a finalist, you'd be assigned a mentor from WWE who would help you prepare for the finals.

"I'm *so* winning this," Alex said confidently, not waiting for Shawn's answer.

Shawn barely heard his friend. The first germ of an idea was starting to form.

Nowhere did it say that the SuperFan had to be a lifelong WWE fan. In fact, nowhere did it say you had to be part of the WWE Universe to enter. That didn't mean you'd win, of course, but it didn't stop you from entering.

Huh.

Shawn thought about how his father would soon be in Afghanistan. He was going because it was the right thing to do for his country. Maybe there was something Shawn could do because it was the right thing to do, too. Not for himself. For his dad.

CHAPTER FOUR

Alex tossed Shawn a white Flip video camera. "Film me. Keep an eye on the clock. This can't be longer than a minute. Not one second longer!"

Shawn nodded. He and Alex had fooled around with the camera a ton of times, so he knew how to use it. "Don't you want to write something out?"

"Nah. I'll wing it. What I miss in prep, I'll make up in enthusiasm. Check it out!" Shawn watched as Alex positioned himself on his bed directly in front of a Rey Mysterio poster—his whole room was a shrine to WWE. Then Alex gave Shawn a sign to start filming.

"Hi, WWE Universe," Alex began. "I'm Alex Garcia, and no one loves the WWE like I do. No one! Look!"

Alex did a thirty-second guided tour of his room as Shawn followed and filmed. "Choose me as SuperFan, and I'll make the WWE proud. Six-one-nine!" Alex finished with Rey Mysterio's signature chant and then thrust his arms overhead in a victory pose.

"Good one," Shawn told him as he stopped the recording. Then he made a decision: If he shot a video of his own, he didn't have to enter SuperFan. But he'd have it just in case.

He tossed the Flip camera to his friend. "Now me," he said quietly.

"What?!"

"I said, now me," Shawn repeated.

Alex look at him, his jaw slack. Then he whooped. "Shawn's gonna enter! I can't believe it! Shawn's gonna enter!"

Shawn sat on the bed, embarrassed. "I'm not sure if I will. But I might. It would mean a lot to my dad."

"Then start talking before you change your mind!"

He pointed the Flip camera at Shawn, who had no idea what to say. "This could take a while, Alex. Like, till we get our driver's licenses."

"Shawn? Shut up and talk."

Shawn nodded, then sat back on Alex's bed and started to talk. Well, not exactly. He sat for three full seconds of silence before he began.

"Hi." He gave a little wave. "My name is Shawn Reynolds, I'm from Columbia, Missouri, and this is my video for SuperFan. I'm not even sure I am going to enter. The truth is, I hated WWE until last night, when I went to a *Raw* show for my little brother's birthday. The truth is, if my father wasn't going to Afghanistan at the end of the week, I don't think I would even think about entering. The truth is, he's a huge WWE fan. I'm not. The truth is, until last night, I didn't really know the difference between John Cena and Sheamus or CM Punk and Rey Mysterio. But I want to make my dad happy, even though the truth is I'm a pretty cruddy athlete. All I can say is that if you pick me, I'll be just like a lot of other kids out there. Probably even most kids out there. We're not the greatest, but we're us."

Shawn glanced at the clock. Fifteen seconds to go, but he had nothing more to say.

"That's it," he added. "Oh! If you don't pick me, pick my friend Alex Garcia."

"Great," Alex declared as he shut down the camera. "Especially the last line. Let's show this to my mom and then tell your dad what's going on. He'll be so psyched!"

"No!" Shawn's reaction was immediate.

"No? Why not?"

"Because, I told you before, I'm not sure if I'm going to enter! And if I do, I want this to be the best surprise my dad has ever gotten."

CHAPTER FIVE

"Morning, Shawnie. Time to get up."

Shawn opened his eyes slowly to see his father sitting at the foot of his bed in his uniform. The sight brought the reality of the day crashing down.

It was three days later. Friday. The day his dad was leaving. The family would drive him to the army base outside St. Louis. From there, his dad would fly to Bagram Airfield near Kabul, Afghanistan. And from there? Shawn tried not to think about that part.

"Got it," Shawn told his dad. He glanced at Peter's empty bed. "Where's Peter?"

"Helping your mom make breakfast. Which, as you know, is no help at all." Peter's lack of skill in the kitchen was another running family joke. No one could make less edible food and leave a worse mess. "Come on, champ. Up you go."

His dad lifted him to his feet. At the *Raw* show in St. Louis, Sanford had bought Peter and Shawn some WWE gear. In honor of his father's departure, Shawn had worn a John Cena T-shirt and boxers to sleep.

Sanford laughed appreciatively. "Nice look. Cena would be proud."

Now is the time to decide. Now.

All week, Shawn had tried to choose whether to enter SuperFan or not. Would his father be impressed, or would he think it was a dumb ploy to make him feel better before he went to Afghanistan? Shawn didn't know. With Alex's help, though, he'd filled out an entry form and saved it to a flash drive. All Shawn would need to do was log on, cut and paste the information, upload the video, and have his dad sign off.

"Can we stop at the computer?" Shawn asked. "There's something I want to check out."

"After we eat," Sanford said a bit sternly as they stepped into the hallway. Shawn knew that his dad hated electronics before breakfast.

"It kind of can't wait. Please?"

His father raised his eyebrows. "It can't wait?"

"It can't wait."

"Fair enough," Sanford agreed. "Five minutes."

The family computer was in the living room. It was far older than Alex's, with a corded mouse. Shawn found it already booted up. Carla usually started her day by checking e-mail. Her American

Library Association coffee cup sat by the mouse pad.

"I'll miss that cup," Sanford mused as Shawn slid into the battered black chair.

Shawn plugged in his flash drive and then clicked the video file. He'd named the file "Mickey Mouse" in case his parents found it by accident.

"We're watching a cartoon?" Sanford asked.

"Not exactly," Shawn responded.

A moment later, his entry video filled the screen, starting with the three silent seconds as he tried to figure out what to say. Then Shawn heard his own voice and saw the little wave he gave to the camera.

"Hi. My name is Shawn Reynolds, I'm from Columbia, Missouri, and this is my video for SuperFan."

"Oh my god, you entered!" Sanford exclaimed.

He watched his dad watching the whole thing until the clip ended and the screen went blank. Shawn closed the media player before he looked up. Oh no. Sanford was frowning.

"Is it okay?" Shawn asked, his voice small.

"It is okay?" His father repeated his words. "Is it okay? My eldest son enters SuperFan. On his entry video he doesn't lie and say he's this big WWE fan. He says he doesn't know the difference between Cena and Sheamus. But he enters, anyway. For me."

Sanford Reynolds was a tough guy. Shawn remembered how three years ago, they'd been in the family car when a careless driver smacked them on the driver's side. His dad's arm had been broken. His dad hadn't cried.

But now? As he gazed at his dad, he saw tears rolling down his father's cheeks. His dad took a camouflage bandanna from his back pocket—he was the only dad Shawn knew who habitually carried a handkerchief—and dabbed at his eyes. Then he forced a sad smile.

"At the right time, Shawn? At the right place? Don't be afraid to cry," Sanford advised. "It doesn't make you less of a man. It makes you more of one."

Shawn nodded. Then his father opened his arms wide, and Shawn got the biggest hug of his young life. "I love you, Shawnie," his dad said in a deep voice.

"I love you, Dad. Please come home safe."

At the right time, Shawn? At the right place? Don't be afraid to cry. It doesn't make you less of a man. It makes you more of one.

This was the right time. The right place. Shawn let the tears come.

★ ★ ★

"Wave to your dad!" Carla instructed the boys.

They stood with several other military families in the main parking area of the National Guard base ten miles west of St. Louis.

"Dad's waving back!" Peter exclaimed.

Shawn saw his father turn around to pick them out in the crowd and give a single wave. Then he shouldered his duffel bag and walked on toward a cluster of low-slung brown buildings. Shawn felt proud and empty at the same time.

The moment Sanford was out of sight, his mother turned businesslike. "Your father wouldn't want us to stand here moping. Let's go home." She started toward their old Pontiac.

Shawn raised his chin at Peter, signaling that this was the time. After breakfast, when Sanford proudly shared the news that Shawn was entering the SuperFan contest, his mom and dad had shared a private moment on the front porch. That was when Shawn took Peter aside and planned what to say to their mom after their dad was gone.

"Just a sec, Mom," Peter called.

Carla stopped. "Yes?"

Shawn fidgeted a little. "We just wanted to say, well, that this is really hard. So Peter and I promise we're not going to make it harder."

"We're not going to argue," Peter promised.

"And we've made up a chores sheet," Shawn went on.

"We'll do our homework without being asked. With a clarion!" Peter got in the last word.

"Peter?" Carla raised her eyebrows. "A clarion is a trumpet. The word you want is *alacrity*."

"Yeah. That, too." Peter agreed. "And if Shawn wins SuperFan? I'll cheer with alacrity! And blow a clarion!"

Carla smiled sadly at her sons. "Thank you, boys. Your father would be proud of you both."

She put out her arms. For the second time that morning, Shawn felt himself embraced in a world-class hug. He told himself that while it was easy to say he'd do his chores and wouldn't fight with his brother, he had to do more than just say those things. He'd have to do them.

I will do them for my mom, the same way I entered SuperFan for my dad, he told himself. *I won't let either of them down.*

CHAPTER SIX

"What's your homework?" Carla asked. She was at the computer, making changes on the library's website of recommended books for boys.

Shawn squirmed. It was two weeks to the day after they'd dropped his dad off at the National Guard base, and he'd just been assigned an oral book report on a novel of his choice. It was a double whammy assignment. First, he was a very slow reader. Second, the idea of standing in front of his class and talking filled him with fear.

"I've got to find a book for an oral report."

Carla saved her work and faced Shawn. "When's it due?"

"In three weeks."

Carla smiled at her son sympathetically. "You hate oral reports. I know that."

"Yeah."

"Do you want help finding a book?" she asked.

"No. Unless you'd like to read it and give the report for me!" Shawn joked.

With Sanford away, the Reynolds house had settled into something of a routine. Carla would get the boys off to school and then go to work.

A lot of times, Mrs. Garcia would invite the boys over on Monday or Friday night, so they could watch *Raw* and *SmackDown* and Carla could go to the movies with friends or do volunteer work at their church. Shawn found watching the Superstars and Divas comforting. It was like a silent connection with his father.

One of the hardest things was e-mail. Carla had decided that they'd look together every night at six thirty. That was before dawn in Afghanistan, a good time for Sanford to get access to a computer at the servicemen's center at his base. Sometimes they could even Skype.

"I'm going to suggest some books, anyway. I think you'll like the ones by Jerry Spinelli."

Carla was starting to jot down some titles when Peter skidded across the wooden floor in his socks. "It's almost six thirty! Is Dad on Skype?"

"It's not quite time," Carla told him.

"We should check, anyway. Maybe Dad's watch is wrong," Peter reasoned.

Shawn rolled his eyes. "Dad's watch is never wrong."

"Well, this could be the first time."

"How about if I give in and we end the mystery?" Carla suggested. She opened Skype. "Nope. He's not online. Let's check e-mail."

"Yes!" Peter exclaimed, once Carla had logged in. "There's a new letter!"

Dear family,

I have to keep this short because there's a line of soldiers who want to use this computer. Am being sent in country on a classified mission. That means I can't tell you where I'm going. I don't know how long I'll be out of touch. I will take care of myself, and your job is to take care of yourselves. Hey! Peter and Shawn! It's Friday night in the States, which means that *SmackDown* is on TV. Why don't you guys watch and tell me about it in your next e-mail? What's the latest with SuperFan, anyway?

Carla, I love you.

DAD

When they all finished reading, the room was so quiet that they could hear the whirring of the computer's fan. Since Sanford had been sent overseas, they knew that at some point his unit would be sent into action. This e-mail told them that the time was now.

"I'm nervous, Mom." Peter said what they all were thinking.

"What about you, Shawn?" Carla asked.

Shawn nodded.

"We're all nervous," Carla declared. "But we have to go on the way Sanford—your dad—would want us to go on."

Shawn had what he hoped was a great idea.

"I think we should still write to him every day. That way, when he comes back from his mission, he'll have a million e-mails to read."

Carla laughed sadly. "I hope not a million. That would be a very long mission."

"Mom, you know what I mean!"

"And you boys know what I mean." Carla stood and stretched. Shawn noticed she was still in one of the pantsuits she wore to the library. She hadn't even had time to change into comfortable clothes. "I've got to get dinner together. What are your plans for tonight? Anything?"

Shawn and Peter answered at the same time. "Watch *SmackDown*!"

★ ★ ★ ★

It was a great night for watching television. Though the weather forecast was for unseasonably warm temperatures tomorrow, tonight the temps were in the low teens with howling winds. Carla invited the Garcias over. They arrived bundled up and with a huge platter of provisions—popcorn, chips, and salsa for the kids, and two fresh pies for the adults. The kids settled down on the living room floor with blankets and pillows to watch *SmackDown*. The adults went into the kitchen to do what adults do, which is to talk endlessly about a lot of boring stuff.

Shawn was looking forward to watching the show. In the last few weeks, he'd become something of a fan. Not a fanatic like Alex or Peter, but definitely a fan. He'd decided it was the combination of entering the SuperFan contest, how his dad's e-mails always seemed to mention WWE, and the fun of coming to know the Superstars, the Divas, and their stories.

SmackDown began; they were broadcasting from Texas, and the announcers touted matches between Kane and Big Show, a tag team contest between the Hart Dynasty and the team of Drew McIntyre and Cody Rhodes, and a Divas three-on-three battle. Before the bell sounded for the first match, though, Mr. McMahon entered the ring.

"Before we begin the action tonight," Mr. McMahon announced, "I wanted to share some news. The WWE has received a record five hundred thousand—I repeat, five hundred thousand!—entries from young WWE fans ready to vie for the title of SuperFan. Every one of these entries has been reviewed by the WWE. We have chosen four remarkable finalists!"

"They know who they are!" Peter exclaimed.

"And I'm one of 'em!" Alex mock-boasted.

Shawn slumped a little. If ever in his wildest dreams he'd thought he had a chance to be a finalist, the number of applicants made it pretty much impossible. He'd be more likely to win the lottery.

Mr. McMahon had more. "The WWE will make an announcement about the four winners on our website tomorrow morning at 10:00 AM eastern standard time. I'll give you a hint, though. There are three boy finalists and one girl. Now, let's get on with *SmackDown*!"

"Three guys and a girl," Alex repeated.

"Yeah," Peter joked. "You're the girl!"

Shawn laughed; Alex jumped on Peter and started to tickle him. Then Shawn jumped on Alex and starting tickling them both, which resulted in legs kicking bowls of chips and popcorn in all directions. It took quite a while to clean up before they settled down to watch. The best part for Shawn was that Rey Mysterio made a surprise appearance.

"I will wrestle CM Punk," he declared, leaning on a cane to support his injured ankle. "I will take him on at a time and place of my choosing. I will make him say 'I quit!' to me! And until then? He's not wrestling!"

Punk wasn't in the arena, but he was again piped in via video, and he happily accepted the challenge. Mysterio could name the time and place. Punk would be there.

As Shawn watched, he wished he could be there, too. He knew that tomorrow morning he'd be logging on to the WWE website. He knew he'd be hoping against hope.

Even though Shawn was starting to feel like part of the WWE Universe, he knew he didn't have a chance. But he knew he'd check it out, anyway.

CHAPTER SEVEN

"One minute!" Peter shouted. "Just a minuscule minute more!"

"Do you think Dad's following this, too?" Shawn wondered aloud.

Carla shook her head thoughtfully. "Ordinarily, I'd say no. But this is your dad we're talking about, and it has to do with WWE and you. I'd say if there's a way to do it, he'll do it."

It was the next morning, a glorious, unseasonably warm day for Missouri in February. Except for Mr. Garcia, who had a crisis at the print shop, everyone had come back to the Reynoldses' for the big announcement of the SuperFan finalists on the WWE website.

"Twenty more seconds." Alex nervously ran a hand through his buzz cut and leaned toward the monitor.

The moments ticked down. At ten seconds, Peter started counting down with the clock. Alex joined in as the numbers dropped. "Five, four . . ."

Shawn couldn't help himself. "Three, two, one. Time!"

The WWE logo flashed colors and spun crazily for a few moments. Then it reset. Obviously, the names of the finalists were about to be posted. Here it came. The list!

Except it wasn't the list. An announcement flashed on the screen against a backdrop of the faces of a dozen or more Superstars and Divas.

SuperFan Finalists to Be Notified in Person Before We Post Their Names Here!

"What does that mean?" Peter didn't understand. "They're not telling us?"

At first, seeing the announcement made Shawn feel like someone was playing a mean game. But it quickly made sense. What if a finalist didn't have a computer? That was possible. That person deserved to find out before the rest of the world. It was actually a considerate thing for the WWE to do.

"We put our phone numbers on the applications," Shawn reminded his brother and Alex. "I bet that's how they're going to notify everyone."

Mrs. Garcia waved her iPhone. "Tons of bars. If they call, I'm ready."

"Or don't call," Shawn commented wryly. It

wasn't like he heard ringing. He tried to muster a brave smile. "Alex, it's not going to be us."

He saw his friend's eyes grow sad. "I know. Well, it was still fun."

"So how about if Isabel and I make some huevos rancheros?" Carla suggested, wanting to lighten the mood. "There are some boys who were too nervous to eat—"

The doorbell interrupted her.

"Mailman, I'm sure. More books, I'm extra sure," Carla declared.

"I'll sign for them," Shawn offered.

"Thanks, Shawnie. You might want to bring a wheelbarrow," his mother joked.

Shawn stepped across the wooden floor of the entry hall as the doorbell chimed again.

"Coming!" he shouted. "One sec!"

He opened the door to find a young man on the doorstep. The guy wasn't a mail carrier. He had short, swept-back dark hair and wore a dark suit and tie.

"Can I help you?" Shawn asked. He'd been taught to be cautious around strangers.

"That depends," the man said warmly. "Are you Shawn Reynolds?"

"I'm him, yeah."

The man extended his right hand. "It's great to meet you. My name is Rodrigo—"

Enough was enough. This was too bizarre. He turned back toward the hallway. "Mom? Can you come here, please?"

When he faced the stranger again, he got the shock of his life. Standing with Rodrigo, dressed casually in jeans and an Aztec-themed T-shirt, was a short, powerfully built man with buzzed hair. Shawn could see his eyes but couldn't see his face because the man wore a multicolored mask that covered his forehead, cheekbones, and nose.

Omigod, Shawn realized. *It's—*

The stranger finished Shawn's thought for him. "Hi, Shawn. I'm Rey Mysterio. You're a SuperFan finalist!"

CHAPTER EIGHT

Rey Mysterio is in my kitchen. Rey Mysterio is in my kitchen. I'm a SuperFan finalist. I'm a SuperFan finalist.

It was true. Otherwise, Rey Mysterio wouldn't be sitting across from Shawn at the kitchen table, flanked by Rodrigo and a WWE cameraman. Otherwise, Peter wouldn't be staring at Rey gape-mouthed, with the two moms standing in a state of shock.

Shawn glanced to his left at Alex, who flashed him two big thumbs-up. That was great. Shawn's first thought, when he had recovered from the disbelief of being chosen, had been that his buddy might be jealous. But that wasn't the case. Alex was genuinely thrilled for him.

Rey kept it brief. "WrestleMania weekend is at the start of your spring break. We're going to fly you, your mom, and your brother to Atlanta. Also, one friend. Any idea who you'd like that to be?"

Shawn nodded vehemently. "Definitely my friend Alex."

"That would be me!" Alex exclaimed.

Rey nodded at Mrs. Garcia. "We can bring you, too, ma'am. Or Ms. Reynolds can chaperone by herself. Let us know." Then he turned back to Shawn. "We'll put you in the same hotel with the Superstars and Divas. You'll have a suite. All expenses handled by the WWE. On the Friday and Saturday before WrestleMania, you'll be in a series of competitions. The winner will be named SuperFan and will carry in the championship at the main event on Sunday afternoon." Rey pushed a packet of information across the table to Shawn. "There's a sheet that lists all the prizes. The college scholarship is the biggest thing."

"It better be," Carla joked, and everyone laughed. When things settled down, Carla had a question for Rey. "What kind of competitions?"

"What I know is that they'll cover the range of what we want in our first SuperFan. Athletic skill, definitely. Endurance, for sure. But also artistic ability, intelligence, and character. You'll also be doing some community service in Atlanta, Shawn."

"I'm not a good athlete," Shawn murmured. He usually finished last in anything involving sports.

"Are you sure? Have you ever trained? I mean, really trained? Day after day the way we Superstars do?" Rey frowned, and his eyes bore into Shawn the way they had against Sheamus in St. Louis.

Shawn shook his head. "No. I've never really trained."

"Then you have no idea what's possible." Rey swung around toward Carla with the fluid movements of a panther. "I understand you're a librarian."

"That's right."

"The WWE loves librarians. You have *The Adventures of Tom Sawyer* in the library, no?"

"Of course."

Shawn raised his eyebrows. Rey read Shawn's expression and pointed at him. "You're going to read it. It's a great book about two boys who are best friends."

"Like Alex and me?" Shawn asked.

"Not exactly," Rey said. Carla and Mrs. Garcia chuckled, which made Shawn think they'd read *Tom Sawyer*. He definitely hadn't. "What's the most number of times you've ever read a book?"

Shawn didn't remember reading anything more than once, which is what he told Rey.

"Read this five times. At least. Know it cold."

Five times? Did Rey Mysterio just tell me to read a book

five times? I can barely get through most books once!

Rey stood, using his cane for leverage, his injured ankle obviously still bothering him. "If it's okay with your mom, Shawn, I'd like to get going on a training routine right away, and bring your brother and Alex along for support. It's warm enough. You do your part, I'll do mine. Got it?"

Shawn nodded. He felt nervous, but who could be a better trainer than Rey Mysterio? "Got it."

"Excellent. Any other questions before we start?"

Peter, who'd been silent this whole time, jumped in. "Do you really hate CM Punk?"

"Let's say we're not best buds." Rey banged his cane on the linoleum for emphasis. "Next question."

"Can I get a guided tour of your tattoos?" Alex queried.

Rey looked taken aback. Then he smiled. "Not right now. My mom taught me that men should always keep their shirts on at the table. Any others?"

Shawn had one, but Peter beat him to it.

"Can we see you without your mask?"

"No." Rey's voice was emphatic. "You're not my wife, you're not my kids, so you don't get to see me without my mask. Next question."

Shawn spoke up. Actually, it was more an idea than a question.

"My dad? He's in Afghanistan. He's out on a mission and won't find out that I'm a finalist till he's back. So I was wondering . . . we send him e-mail and stuff. Can we maybe make him a video so he'll see it when he gets back to his base? He's like the biggest WWE fan ever. The only thing is . . ."

Rey raised his eyebrows at Shawn's hesitation.

Shawn was too embarrassed to continue. Alex, though, felt no embarrassment. "Shawn's dad? His favorite Superstar is Cena."

Rey burst out laughing. "Well, then. I'll just have to change his mind." He dug in his jeans pocket for his BlackBerry. "I love that idea. How about if we shoot it right now. On this?"

The WWE cameraman wanted to keep filming, so Mrs. Garcia volunteered to be in charge of the BlackBerry. Rey gathered everyone on one side of the kitchen table, with Mrs. Garcia on the other. He put Shawn front and center. "Okay, Señora Garcia. Wave when you're ready."

Mrs. Garcia waved. Rey spoke first. "Hello, Mr. Reynolds, serving our country overseas. I wish

I could say my name was John Cena, but I'm Rey Mysterio, and I'm coming to you live from your family's kitchen. Shawn and Peter, say 'Hi, Dad!' so your father knows this is legit."

"Hi, Dad!" the boys called together.

"I'm bringing you awesome news. Your son Shawn is one of the four WWE SuperFan finalists, and my job is to get him in shape to win. Win or lose—and my goal is to help him win—I think that when you come home you're going to see a very different Shawn Reynolds. Thank you for your service. As proud as you must be of Shawn right now, we're all doubly proud of you. Booyaka, 619!"

Perfect, Shawn thought. *Dad will love that.*

Shawn suddenly felt Rey turn him in the direction of the living room. "Put on a T-shirt, shorts, socks, and some kind of gym shoes," his mentor instructed. "You, too, Peter. Alex, we'll stop at your house so you can change. Let's go! We've got work to do!"

CHAPTER NINE

"Hurting, Shawn?" Rey called down from the top of the bleachers.

"Yeah!" Shawn managed. What he didn't say was, "Of course I'm hurting! I hate to run! I hate sports!" That didn't mean he wasn't thinking it.

"Run through the pain, man!" Rey insisted. Shawn was not going to quit on Rey Mysterio. He kept climbing the football stadium steps. Five more. Five more, even as Alex and Peter reached the top and got high-fives from Rey so loud that Shawn could hear. Shawn slowed but kept going. Then he was walking. Just a little bit more . . .

That was it. His legs gave out; his heart felt like it was about to blow through his rib cage. He slumped on a bleacher, wrapped his arms around his bare lower legs, and sucked wind.

"What's going on, Shawn?" Rey shouted. "You're just halfway up!"

"I'm tired!"

"Of course you're tired, that's why you're

training! Come. Up. Those. Stairs!"

Shawn wanted to keep going. He was willing. But his legs and lungs weren't willing. He tried one more step. Not happening.

"Okay, Shawn! We're coming down."

Great. Lucky me. Humiliated. I bet he's sorry they picked me.

Shawn put his head in his hands. Two hours earlier, the four of them, plus Rodrigo, the driver, and the cameraman, had taken the stretch limo to the local high school football field. None of the boys had ever been in a limo before; they'd marveled at the plush seats, the refrigerator filled with bottled water and juices, and the entertainment center with the flat-screen TV. The most fun was gazing out the tinted windows at the surprised faces they passed on the sidewalks. Stretch limos in Columbia, Missouri, weren't common. People were wondering who was inside.

The drive had taken only ten minutes; they'd found the field empty. Shawn didn't mind. He was happy that Rey asked the cameraman and Rodrigo to stay with the limo for this first workout. Fewer people would see what a dreadful athlete he was.

They'd started out with simple equipment that Rey pulled from the back of the limo: jump ropes, elastic bands in various lengths and thicknesses, tennis balls, and dumbbells. Rey showed the boys that with these inexpensive tools, you didn't need a fancy gym for a solid workout. Then he taught Shawn a martial arts form to use to center his balance. From there, he brought the boys into the stadium and had them leap from bleacher to bleacher to build agility. After that, he demonstrated simple stretches for their biceps, pecs, glutes, and hamstrings.

Finally, he had them run the stadium steps. That was where Shawn nearly keeled over.

"Hey, SuperFan-to-be," Rey said softly as he approached, trailed by Alex and Peter. It had taken him quite a while to hobble down the stairs with his cane. He offered Shawn a bottle of water, which Shawn drank gratefully. "How do you feel?"

Shawn made a face. "I couldn't even get halfway."

"Not today. Maybe tomorrow. Or the day after that. You'll make it to the top if you train every day. No excuses."

"No excuses," Peter promised. "Or I'll kick my brother's buttocks."

Rey peered closely at Shawn. "Alex and Peter, can you guys run back to the limo? Ask Rodrigo for the white binders and bring them back?"

Shawn smiled. If Rey had asked them to crawl to the limo on their hands and knees they would have been willing.

"You're quiet," Rey observed when the boys were gone. "What are you thinking?"

"How I suck."

"You don't suck. You're just starting."

Shawn shook his head angrily, but his voice was matter-of-fact. "Peter is two years younger than me, and he can run faster and jump higher. He's right. In a fight, he'd kick my butt. About the only things I'm better at than him are art and guitar. Alex is a great athlete and knows way more about WWE than me. I think maybe the WWE goofed."

Shawn still couldn't look Rey in the eyes. "Look at me," Rey commanded, his dark eyes intense.

Shawn looked up.

"I want you to do one thing," Rey demanded. "Take those poison thoughts and stick them where the sun doesn't shine. Can you do that for me?"

Once again, Shawn was honest. He didn't say yes. "I can try."

Rey nodded as Alex started up the bleachers with the white binders in hand. "If you try your hardest, that's good enough for me."

"These weigh a ton!" Alex exclaimed. He carried two of the white binders while Peter handled the other one.

"Playbooks," Rey said knowledgeably.

Shawn had no idea what he was talking about. "Huh?"

Rey took a binder from Alex and handed it to Shawn. "Football players have playbooks with their team's plays. This is your WWE playbook. Alex and Peter have theirs so they can test you."

"There aren't plays in wrestling!" Peter exclaimed.

"True," Rey acknowledged. "But there's a ton to learn, especially if you haven't been a fan for very long. Shawn, memorize this."

"Memorize it?" Shawn was aghast.

"Memorize it," Rey repeated. "When you're not doing schoolwork or volunteer work or training or reading *Tom Sawyer*, that is."

Shawn was about to ask when Rey expected him to sleep, but thought better of it and flipped through the binder. There were hundreds of pages covering WWE history, wrestlers, matchups and rivalries, matches and moves.

"I'm supposed to know all this?" Shawn was incredulous.

"Yep," Rey said.

"You know everything in here?" Shawn challenged.

Rey laughed. "I know all the parts about me. Come on, let's head back to the limo."

The scene that greeted them in the parking lot was far different from when they'd first gotten there. They'd arrived to an empty parking lot. Now, the limo was surrounded by vans with antennae on their roofs and a gaggle of adults. The crowd was shouting questions at Rodrigo.

"Who *are* these people?" Alex exclaimed. "They weren't here before."

Rey smiled wryly. "Word must be out."

"Reporters?" Alex guessed.

"You're a cerebralty, Shawn!" Peter exclaimed.

"Celebrity. And no, I'm not. I'm just a kid," Shawn countered.

"Actually, Shawn, you're gonna be at least a little famous." Rey reset the mask on his face. "Gotta look my best with the media."

Shawn felt stage fright creep up his chest. "I don't want to be interviewed!"

"I'm not sure you have a choice," Alex observed. "Here they come!"

Alex was right. The journalists were in a dead run, and everyone was shouting questions.

"How does it feel to be a finalist, Shawn?"

"Are you named for Shawn Michaels?"

"Do you think you can win?"

"Is it true your father's in Afghanistan?"

"Who's your favorite wrestler?"

"Who's your friend?"

"Who's the other friend? He looks like your brother. How come he's so big and you're so small? Who's older?"

The questions kept coming. Shawn felt close to panic. But Rey was used to dealing with reporters. He whispered to Shawn. "I'll talk. When I turn to you, say, 'I'm just proud to be a part of the competition.' Got it?"

Shawn nodded. It wasn't like he could come up with something to say on his own.

"Quiet, please! Quiet!" Rey held up a beefy arm for silence, and the crowd hushed. "I'm Rey Mysterio. I'll make a brief statement, then Shawn will make a brief statement, and then we need to go so the boys can do their homework. Middle school is killer."

The reporters laughed. Rey already had them charmed.

"Shawn Reynolds is a worthy finalist, and I'm thrilled to be his WWE mentor," Rey continued. "We want our first SuperFan to be an athlete and a scholar, a good friend and a good person, strong of mind, body, and heart. Will Shawn win? I don't know. But you guys can help him by giving him the space he needs. Shawn, can you say a few words?"

Shawn gulped. This was his cue. But there were cameras. Was any of this live?

Probably not, he reasoned. *Not in the middle of the day on a Saturday. But still.*

He managed to croak out the sentence Rey had given him to say. "I'm just proud to be a part of the competition. Thank you."

"Can't hear you!" a tall, skinny female reporter shouted at him.

"Is that it?" Another writer frowned.

The reporters' questions and complaints came fast and furious, but Rey took over again.

"Gotta go!" Then he turned to the boys. "Hustle outta here."

The kids dashed for the limo and scrambled in, with Rey following as quickly as his bum ankle would allow.

"Welcome to the big time," Rey declared as the limo pulled away.

"You're a star, Shawn!" Peter was awestruck by what had just happened.

"I don't want to be a star!" Shawn moaned.

"Good. Don't think about that. Think about this." Rey picked up the remote control for the flat-screen TV and pressed a few buttons. "This is what I wanted you to see. Who you're up against."

Huh. His opponents. So much had happened since Rey rang his doorbell that Shawn hadn't even thought about who his competition would be in Atlanta.

That changed in a hurry as Rey started the entry videos of Shawn's three rivals. There was DeJuan Smith, an African American boy from Baltimore, Maryland, whom Shawn liked immediately. DeJuan was funny, energetic, and did a perfect imitation of Sheamus's voice as part of his video. He'd be mentored by former champion The Miz. The girl was Jayden Starr from Los Angeles, California. Jayden had somehow recorded her video in a wrestling ring while she did gymnastics across the floor. Like DeJuan, she seemed cool.

"Her mentor is Natalya. She's been the Divas Champion. Very beautiful, very tough. Now check out the last one." Rey frowned.

Up came a video from a kid named Spike Murcer. Spike was from Renton, Washington. He was tall, he was wide, and he was strong. Spike had shot his video in a gym and did bicep curls with heavy dumbbells as he talked. "I want to grow up to be a WWE Superstar. The best way to do that is to be the first SuperFan. That's why I'm going to win. And everyone else is going to lose."

Shawn shuddered a bit. There was nothing that Spike was saying that was so bad, but he just had a feeling about the guy. Plus, there were those huge dumbbells.

The video ended as the limo stopped in front of Shawn's house. "Who's his mentor?" Shawn asked.

"His mentor?" Rey repeated. "Funny you should ask that. It's my favorite person in the world: CM Punk."

Shawn gulped. "Can you play it again?"

Rey reran the video. Amazing. Spike even looked like Punk, with dark hair and brooding eyes. He had Punk's cocky mouth and slight sneer. All he was missing were Punk's famous tattoos.

Shawn shuddered. These were the kids he'd have to beat. But how?

CHAPTER TEN

"Hey, it's the SuperFan!"

"Nah, it's not the SuperFan. Shawn Reynolds'll never be the SuperFan!"

"Well, then. It's the SuperFraud!"

Shawn's ears burned as he took his place in the batter's box of the Columbia East Middle School baseball diamond. It was two weeks after Rey Mysterio had shown up on his doorstep. Two weeks of exercising in the snow, rain, or shine, of studying the white binder with Peter and Alex, and of reading and rereading *Tom Sawyer*. Literally every moment that Shawn wasn't doing schoolwork or his chores, he was preparing for the competition. The only thing he did to relax was play his guitar.

Rey monitored his progress by e-mail and made changes to his training routine. To build upper-body strength, he told Shawn to put a pull-up bar in his doorway and use it morning and night. To build balance, Rey had Shawn stand on one leg while Peter and Alex tried to push him over. Two days ago, he'd finally made it to the top of the football bleachers without having to stop.

There was one extra-good part to training that Shawn hadn't anticipated: It distracted him from the fact that they still hadn't heard from his father. Carla assured the boys that this was totally normal, but that didn't make it easier. Shawn still sent daily e-mails so Sanford would come back to a full inbox.

Now it was mid-March and, again, unseasonably warm. The gym teacher, Mr. Marotta, had decreed that they'd play kickball outdoors.

As Shawn waited for Mr. Marotta to take the mound, mean cracks kept coming from the other team. The worst came from Jeff Harrison, who was both a terrible student and the class bully.

"Yo, Weenie Shawn!" Jeff was shouting from left field. "The only ring you belong in is a ring-around-the-rosy. *Ashes, ashes, Shawn falls down!*"

Jeff tumbled to the ground, flailing his arms and legs. His teammates cracked up.

Shawn gritted his teeth. Rey had warned him that part of being a celebrity—and Shawn was definitely now a mini-celebrity—was that some people would want to knock you down just because they could. Jeff Harrison was one of those people.

It wasn't all bad, though. Other kids were extra friendly now that he was a SuperFan finalist. Some of them would never even give him the time of day before. It was flattering, but it made Shawn really grateful for a true friend like Alex, who'd be his friend no matter how the competition turned out.

"Hey, Weenie! Why'd they pick you? I know! Because they wanted two boys and two girls!" Jeff pranced around the outfield like a fashion model. "Spike Murcer's going to smush you!"

Shawn stewed. He didn't even like to think about Spike Murcer, who'd recently posted a whole series of videos about himself and his greatness on the WWE website. When was Mr. Marotta gonna pitch? As usual, Shawn had been the last one picked when sides were chosen. Wouldn't it feel great to smash one way over Jeff Harrison's annoying head? Maybe he could pretend that Jeff was Spike.

Could he do it? After all these workouts, he was stronger. But feeling stronger and smacking one past the pitcher's mound were two different things.

As if to highlight that fact, Jeff danced in from left field until he stood with the shortstop. "Weenie Boy SuperFraud can't kick it over an anthill!"

More mean laughter. Meanwhile, Shawn's

teammates were silent. Apparently they didn't have much confidence in Shawn, either.

Finally, Mr. Marotta came to the mound. "Ready, Shawn?"

"Bring it," Shawn told him. "And no slow balls."

Shawn knew that even with his training, if he were going to send one into the outfield, the pitch would have to come with pace. Mr. Marotta fired a speedy roll along the ground. Shawn zeroed in on it and kicked as hard as he could.

He missed. Just like in Jeff's obnoxious nursery-rhyme chant, he promptly fell down. Jeff's team howled with laughter, and Jeff did a dead-on imitation of Shawn's wipeout.

"*Ashes, ashes, Shawnie falled-ed down!*" Jeff chortled.

"One more strike, Shawn," Mr. Marotta reminded him as the catcher threw the ball back.

"Same thing." Shawn was grim.

"If you say so." Mr. Marotta rolled the ball toward Shawn again, maybe even faster.

Shawn glanced at Jeff Harrison, who was right behind the shortstop, pretending to be asleep. *Man! How good it would feel if . . .*

With three running steps, Shawn swung with his right foot, trying to angle his kick toward left field.

Boom!

All those stadium steps paid off. The rubber ball exploded off his foot, heading toward left field like a red rocket. By the time Jeff Harrison figured out what was going on, the ball was heading for the fence. He turned and gave chase as Shawn's teammates screamed at him, "Run, Shawn, run!"

Shawn was in such shock that he hadn't budged from the batter's box. With a start, he bolted toward first base.

"Run, Shawn!" his teammates urged. As Shawn rounded first and headed toward second, he could see that Jeff was only now approaching the ball. "Run!"

Shawn bore in on third. Jeff fired the ball to the third baseman. *Safe!* Shawn came in standing up as his teammates shouted with glee.

It was amazing. He'd never made so much as a single before. If he'd run the moment he'd kicked it, he would have had a home run. If only Alex were in his gym class and could have seen this. Well he'd have to tell him all about it.

Mr. Marotta called out approvingly, "Nice shot, Shawn!"

"Thanks!" Shawn called back, still a little dazed.

"Total luck! He couldn't do it again in a million years!" Jeff scoffed and kicked at the dirt.

Shawn didn't know whether what Jeff said was true or not, but it didn't matter. He'd done it once, right here, right now. It felt great. If this was what SuperFan was doing for him, he was loving it.

✳ ✳ ✳ ✳

"Show of hands—how many of you have finished your book for your book report? Oral reports begin next Friday! Has anyone finished yet?" Mrs. Wolfenbarger stared at her class.

Shawn looked around the English 7-A classroom. He was on his fourth reading of *Tom Sawyer,* but if no one else was going to raise their hand, he sure wouldn't.

Not a hand went up.

"No one?" Mrs. Wolfenbarger was obviously unhappy. She was the most senior teacher on the middle school faculty and had the gray hair and tough attitude that came with that status. Shawn liked her, though. All she wanted was for her students to do their work and do it well. "Not a single person?"

No one. Most of the kids got really busy studying their desktops.

Mrs. Wolfenbarger marched to the whiteboard. "Gee. That's too bad. Because if you can prove you've read the book by now, I'll give you an A and you won't have to do the report.

The class gasped as their teacher wrote an *A* on the whiteboard and circled it. "That's how much I hate letting work go until the last minute."

Shawn was stunned. Did Mrs. Wolfenbarger just say that there was a way for him not to do an oral report?

Before he could change his mind, he flung his right hand skyward.

"Shawn Reynolds, yes?"

"Mrs. Wolfenbarger, I'm reading *Tom Sawyer* for my report. I mean, I've finished it."

Jeff Harrison, who sat in the back of the classroom, protested immediately. "That is totally unfair. That's the book he has to read for SuperFan!"

The teacher glared at Jeff. "Jeff, did I call on you?"

"No."

"Then cease the verbal diarrhea. I don't recall ever saying that you couldn't read the same book for two purposes. Did I say that, Jeff?"

"Nopers."

"Excuse me? A word in actual English?"

"No, ma'am," Jeff muttered.

"Exactly. In your case, it might be nice to read a single book for a single purpose—namely, this book report. And it might be nice for it to be at least one reading level up from *The Cat in the Hat*. So, let's see whether Shawn has, as he claims, read *Tom Sawyer*."

She spun back around, faced Shawn, and fired off a string of questions. "Who wrote the book? What was the author's real name? Where did Tom and Becky find themselves toward the end of the story? What was the name of Tom's best friend? What did Tom get the other kids to paint?"

Yikes. Shawn felt anxiety flood the pit of his stomach. This wasn't the same thing as giving an oral report, where he had to stand in front of his class and talk for ten minutes. But it was almost as bad.

When he spoke, he was so nervous that he barely even stopped between the sentences. "*Tom Sawyer* was written by Mark Twain. The author's real name was Samuel Clemens. Tom's best friend is Huckleberry Finn. Tom gets the other kids to paint a fence. Near the end, he and the girl named Becky get lost in a cave."

For a moment, Mrs. Wolfenbarger stood in silence. Then she went back to the whiteboard and re-circled the letter *A*.

"Congratulations, Shawn. That's your grade. Even if you could have enunciated better. And class? If it took SuperFan and WWE to get Shawn to prepare like this?" Her eyes flitted from face to face. "I advise all of you to become wrestling fans."

As six thirty approached, Shawn was noodling around on his guitar and thinking back on his awesome day. An almost home run. An A from the English teacher famous for never giving an A. The only thing that could be better would be if—

A knock on his open door pulled Shawn back to reality. He looked up; his mother stood in the doorway. "Shawn? Are you busy?"

"Not really." He put his guitar aside. His mother hadn't asked him to play for her in a long time, and he didn't want her to ask now.

"Good. I thought maybe we'd check e-mail a little early. It can't hurt, can it?"

"Sounds good. Where's Peter?"

Carla chucked her chin back toward the living

room. "Already waiting. Come on."

Shawn followed his mother to the computer in the living room. What he saw brought a huge lump to his throat. His father was smiling into a webcam, connected to them by Skype.

"Hi, Dad!" Shawn exclaimed as soon as he was in range.

"Hello, SuperFan!" His father laughed with joy. The connection was awesome. His father could have been in the same room, instead of half a world away. "I'm back at base. It's good to see you!"

"Are you okay? What was it like? Did you read all the e-mails? Did you see Rey's video? Did you—"

His father grinned and held up a hand. "Hold on. One at a time! Yes, I've seen the video. And yes, I've read all the e-mails. And now, I'd like to see your mom and brother in the same picture. Squeeze in, okay?"

They did, with Carla in the center and the boys flanking her. They held that position for a full twenty seconds until Sanford offered a gentle wave.

"I love you, guys," he said simply. "Okay. We've got fifteen minutes. I want to hear everything. Talk fast!"

CHAPTER ELEVEN

"Students, faculty, and staff. This is a momentous day. Never before has a student brought us so much positive attention. Tonight, he leaves for Atlanta, and WrestleMania XXVII. Welcome to Shawn Reynolds Day at Columbia East Middle School!"

Huge cheers filled the auditorium at the principal's greeting. Shawn gazed out at the packed auditorium. During the last few weeks, the kids who had been jealous or mean to him seemed to have come around to his side. Even Jeff Harrison. Now he couldn't change classes without kids wishing him good luck. In some odd way, his status as a finalist had brought his school together.

What if he came back a loser? He didn't want to find out.

Mr. Kwan waited for silence and then continued. "I just know that Shawn's going to make us all proud! Now, please turn your attention to this video."

The lights dimmed, and Shawn's classmates started hooting and hollering. The video was hosted by the SuperFan mentors—Rey and Natalya got cheers from the crowd, while Punk and The Miz earned boos—and featured segments on the four finalists, WWE's WrestleMania reading competition, and great moments from WrestleManias past.

It ended with a surprise. Rey Mysterio had recorded a special segment just for Shawn's school where he talked about how much he'd enjoyed working with Shawn.

"How far can Shawn go?" Rey asked. "I can tell you with confidence that your classmate has worked his butt off. Shawn? I'm proud of you, buddy. See you in Atlanta! Booyaka, 619!"

The video ended, and the students went wild. Shawn leaned toward his mother and brother. "I wish Dad could have seen that."

"Me too," Carla said sadly. They'd been in close touch with Sanford, who was spending a lot more time at his base. His dad had said the odds looked really good that he would be able to watch WrestleMania with his friends, and even Skype with the family while they were in Atlanta.

The cheering went on. Shawn saw Alex jumping and waving his arms. Alex's mother was letting him travel to Atlanta alone with the Reynoldses. His

English teacher was applauding. His gym teacher was pumping his fist. Even Jeff Harrison was clapping his hands rhythmically. Principal Kwan let the celebration go on for quite a while. Then, from somewhere near Jeff Harrison—maybe Jeff himself started it, Shawn couldn't tell—a chant started.

"Speech! Speech! Speech!"

Oh no.

The chant spread through the student body like a virus, touching everyone and everything. "Speech! Speech!"

A speech? No! No speech! No speech! I'd rather go one-on-one with Sheamus in a Tables Match. I'd rather they were chanting, "Weenie!"

Principal Kwan grinned and made his way over to Shawn. His mother and brother looked at him with concern. They knew all about his stage fright.

"What do you say, Shawn?" Principal Kwan was full of enthusiasm. "Make this a day they'll never forget!"

His mother caught his eye with a look that Shawn read as, *Do you want me to step in?* Shawn shook his head no. His mother talking to the principal for him? Ugh. Way too humiliating. Then, before Shawn knew what was happening, Principal Kwan was beckoning him to his feet. Shawn's reluctance looked more like modesty than fear, and it inspired more cheers.

Slowly, he approached the podium. His legs felt like jelly.

Don't barf, he told himself.

Luckily, Shawn didn't barf. But as Principal Kwan positioned the microphone, he took a couple of deep breaths that quickly turned into gasps. Shawn was sure everyone in the auditorium could hear, and see, the trickles of sweat he felt beading on his forehead.

His classmates were quiet now. The silence was overwhelming. The faces blurred.

Form words, Shawn told himself. *Remember what Rey told you to say to the media.*

What had Rey told him? He couldn't remember. He heard nervous laughter.

Say something!

He tried to say, "Thank you for coming."

Nothing came out.

CLANG-CLANG! CLANG-CLANG! CLANG-CLANG!

A collective, disappointed "awww" rolled through the auditorium at the sound of the bells that announced the change of classes. Principal Kwan strode to the microphone and eased Shawn to one side. "Students, that's the end of the assembly. Proceed to your second-period classes."

Shawn knew he had been saved by the bell. As his classmates filed out noisily, he also knew that he'd been exactly what Jeff Harrison had called him on the kickball field a few short weeks ago.

Weenie.

★ ★ ★ ★

Undertaker's entrance music, "The Ministry of Darkness," blasted through huge speakers as seventy-five thousand WWE fans jammed into the Georgia Dome in Atlanta for WrestleMania. Undertaker was scheduled to wrestle his brother, Kane, in this main event, and Shawn knew it wasn't going to be a typical match. Not only would the loser have to quit wrestling and never come back, but the loser agreed to be the winner's towel boy, toilet clean-up dude, and sweat-mopper-upper for the rest of his life. It would be decades of utter humiliation, and the whole WWE Universe knew it.

Shawn was in Undertaker's locker room. As SuperFan, he'd get to carry in the championship for Undertaker. He'd been outfitted in a smaller version of Undertaker's black costume. He loved how it looked on him, but he loved how easily he'd defeated DeJuan, Jayden, and Spike even more. His father was watching on television in Afghanistan. His family and Alex had front-row seats. Could anything be more exciting?

CLANG-CLANG! Through a speaker hookup, Shawn heard the ring bell sound. Time for the match.

"You're up, Shawn! Go get 'em, SuperFan!" People shouted encouragement. Someone pressed the championship into his hands. Shawn raised it over his head, loving the feel of the leather and admiring the glint of the lights off the engraved metal.

"Ready, Shawn? Lead me out there!" Undertaker called to him, looking like a human mountain in his robe. Then the lights were flashing, the fog machines were pumping out smoke, and the indoor fireworks were exploding in bursts of white and green.

"Members of the WWE Universe, please welcome to the Georgia Dome, representing Undertaker, our very first SuperFan, Shawn Reynolds!"

As seventy-five thousand people rose as one, Shawn walked into the arena, his arms thrust skyward, the championship held high overhead.

The cheers suddenly stopped. People started

pointing. Shawn whirled, thinking that someone might be coming up behind him. Someone like Spike, to try to hurt him the way that CM Punk had hurt Rey Mysterio.

Nothing. But the cheers had turned to laughter. Rolling waves of laughter rocked the arena. What was so funny? People were laughing so hard, they were pounding their hands and stomping their feet; Shawn could feel the vibrations right through his bare feet and—

Bare feet? Where were his boots? Shawn looked down. No boots. Not just no boots, but no clothes! He was out there absolutely naked!

He tried to flee, but his feet were stuck, and he couldn't move. The laughter went on.

"No!" he cried. "No, no, no, no, no—"

"Shawn! Shawn!"

Shawn felt someone shaking his arm.

"Wha-what? Where am I?" He could still hear the evil laughter.

It was Alex. "Dude! We're almost in Atlanta. You were having a nightmare, I think."

"Yeah." He'd been dreaming, for sure.

"Look outside. We're landing in fifteen minutes. It's absolutely amazing!"

Shawn was in the window seat; he peered out at the city lights that sprawled beneath them. "Yeah."

He knew he should be excited, but that nightmare had really gotten to him. What did it mean? Was it a warning to himself that he was heading into a situation that could only result in horrible embarrassment?

"What were you dreaming about?" Alex pressed.

Shawn shook his head. "It doesn't matter. I'm okay."

As the landing gear lowered, he knew he'd just lied. Shawn was anything but okay. In fact, he was wondering if entering SuperFan was the biggest mistake of his life.

Shawn found himself pulled to the left and right simultaneously by his brother and Alex. "Whoa! Look over there!" Alex yanked at his left arm. "That's The Miz!"

"That's nothing!" Peter shouted. "Look who just came in! Kofi Kingston and Randy Orton! And over by the escalator! It's all the guys from the New Nexus! And The Corre. And Dolph Ziggler!"

It was an hour and a half later, and Shawn and his family were checking in at their hotel downtown. Most of the Superstars and Divas were staying there, plus celebrities who had come for the weekend. At that moment, Shawn stood toward the front of a quick-moving line with his mother, Alex, Peter, and Rodrigo, the same WWE employee who had accompanied Rey to Shawn's house that exciting day ten weeks ago. Again, Rodrigo wore a coat and tie; an official WWE credential hung around his neck. He'd met them at the Atlanta airport.

"Anything you need, I'm your go-to guy," he'd

told them. "My job is to make it easy for Shawn."

True to his word, Rodrigo had gathered their bags, led them to a black town car idling in the pick-up area, and drove with them to the hotel. Once they were there, he delivered their bags to the bell desk. When their turn came to check in, he signed everything and handed over the key cards. All they had to do was follow him to the elevator. "The other finalists are already here," he reported.

"Are they on our floor?" Carla asked.

Rodrigo smiled. "They are. Four suites, and you competitors have all four."

Shawn hesitated. "Where's Rey? I thought he was meeting us."

Rodrigo wiggled a finger at Shawn. "Patience, SuperFan. If Rey said he's meeting you, he's meeting you."

Five minutes later, they'd exited the elevator and walked past the ice machine to their suite at the far end of the twentieth floor. As they neared the heavy wooden door, Rodrigo happily rattled off the various hotel amenities: weight room, pool, game room, spa, in-room movies and video games, plus twenty-four-hour room service. Shawn and his group could use any and all of it, paid for by the WWE.

Rodrigo swung the door open. "Enjoy this."

Shawn stared. The Reynolds family had only ever stayed in budget motels on road trips to visit relatives. A Holiday Inn was a splurge.

There's nothing wrong with the Holiday Inn, but this was a palace!

From the front hallway, Shawn could see a living room and dining room done in green and white, plus a tiled kitchen. One wall was floor-to-ceiling glass. Downtown Atlanta shimmered before their eyes. To his pleasant surprise, there was an acoustic guitar propped up on a stand to one side of the couch. He'd mentioned in his application that he played guitar. WWE had thought of everything.

"The Georgia Dome is to the left," Rodrigo added helpfully. "There are three bedrooms. Carla, you'll find a hot tub and steam shower in the master bath."

Carla raised her eyebrows quizzically. "A steam shower? The only steam shower I ever take is when the bathroom fan is broken. Who normally stays here?"

"Rock stars, mostly," Rodrigo responded. "And athletes." He turned to the boys. "Two of you are going to have to share a room."

Shawn had already thought about that. Peter

had never, ever had the experience of sleeping in his own room. What better first time than now?

When Peter heard Shawn's plan, he couldn't thank Shawn enough. "I'm appreciation."

Shawn smiled. "It's appreciative, and yes, you are."

They spent the next few minutes getting settled. Peter whooped when he saw the queen bed, and he whooped again at his own bathroom. Shawn was fine to share a room with Alex. He dived onto his bed and stretched his arms out, the nightmare temporarily forgotten. "I could get used to this."

"Don't." Carla issued a mock warning. "Unless you're planning to be very, very rich. Which means you should definitely not be a soldier or a children's librarian."

"Shawn?" Rodrigo came up behind his mom. "You've got a visitor."

Shawn went to the living room, then beamed when he saw who was at the door. Rey Mysterio. He was dressed casually in jeans, a white button-down shirt, and a black leather motorcycle jacket, yet he still wore a black wrestling mask. No cane, thank goodness.

"Hey, hey!" Rey welcomed Shawn. "It's the

future SuperFan. What do you think of your home away from home?" He extended his arms as if he were personally responsible for the gorgeous suite.

"It's . . . it's the nicest place I've ever stayed," Shawn admitted.

"You win SuperFan? You'll get to stay in a lot of nice hotels." He laughed. "Probably not like this, though. You know the schedule for tomorrow?"

They sat together on the biggest couch, and Rey went over the schedule. The first challenge would happen in the Dome at ten. Rodrigo needed everyone downstairs at a quarter to nine. Rey recommended a room-service breakfast.

"Do you know what the event is going to be?" Shawn asked.

"No clue, buddy," Rey told him with a shrug. "Be ready for anything."

Shawn gulped. *Easier said than done,* he thought.

"Your ankle is better." Shawn shifted the subject away from himself.

Rey nodded. "Much. I'm not quite ready for the ring, though." He frowned. "We'll see Punk tomorrow. That'll be entertaining."

"What are you going to do?" Shawn didn't want Rey to get into a fight.

"Not sure. But I know what you're going to do." Rey looked right at Shawn. "Beat Spike Murcer. I can't wait to see Punk's ugly face when that happens." Rey's BlackBerry chimed, and he smiled as he checked the text. "It's my wife and kids—they're here with me. Alia—my daughter—wants her bedtime story. I gotta run. See you at the Dome." He offered Shawn a fist bump, and then Shawn walked him to the door.

Afterward, with Rey gone, Shawn went for a drink. The fridge was stocked with every beverage known to mankind, but no ice cubes. Shawn asked his mom if he could go down the hall to the ice machine. Carla said it was fine.

It only took a few seconds for Shawn to fill the metal bucket with tiny, round cubes. As he turned to head back, he heard his named called from behind.

"Shawn! Shawn Reynolds!" The voice was a kid's, but an octave lower than his own.

Shawn's heart lurched as he took in who'd called his name. Shawn would have recognized him anywhere: Spike Murcer. He wore gym shorts and a white T-shirt. He was easily six inches taller than Shawn and had to outweigh him by at least fifty pounds. He still looked a lot like a junior CM Punk.

"So." Spike cleared his throat to draw out the

moment. "The great Shawn Reynolds. You don't look so great. In fact, I have to say you look a lot like a weenie."

Shawn's ears burned. Spike had just called him what Jeff Harrison used to call him. Had Spike been spying on the kickball game? Doubtful. Maybe Shawn just gave off a weenie aura or something. He knew he should say something. But what?

"You're Spike, right?"

Spike nodded. "Yep, Weenie. I'm Spike. And I have only one thing to say to you. Out of all the competitors, I hate you the most."

"H-hate me?" Shawn sputtered. "You don't even know me!"

"I know I don't know you. But I still hate you. If I were you I'd watch your back. I'd watch your front. And I'd watch your sides." Spike edged closer to him. "I saw your video. You don't even like WWE."

"I do, too!" Shawn defended himself. He was an official part of the WWE Universe now.

"No, you're a poser. And you're a weenie. Know what, Weenie? By this time tomorrow, there won't be any weenies in the competition. Bye, WW-Weenie!"

With that, Spike turned away. Shawn stood there, quaking.

Spike Murcer had just totally psyched him out.

CHAPTER THIRTEEN

"Shawn! Come quick! Your father's on Skype!"

It was the next morning—the morning of the first challenge. Everyone was up early. Peter had been so excited that Shawn heard him padding around the living room at five o'clock.

Thankfully, even after the Spike Murcer psych-out, Shawn had slept well. The bed was so comfortable he'd fallen asleep moments after his head had hit the pillow.

The plan had been for Carla to order a room-service breakfast. Though his father's recent e-mails had mentioned the possibility of a Skype call, and there was an excellent computer in the suite with Wi-Fi and a webcam, Shawn was still surprised. He ran from the shower to join his mother and brother.

Sure enough, his father's face was on the monitor.

"Hi, Dad!"

"Hi, SuperFan! It's great to see you. How are you feeling?"

"I'm . . . okay."

"You sound nervous."

"I am," Shawn admitted.

Sanford rubbed his freshly shaved chin. "Only a potted plant wouldn't be nervous. Make the nerves work for you. What's the challenge today?"

Shawn shook his head. "No one knows."

"Then no one has an advantage. How about the other contestants? I don't like the looks of that Spike guy."

"Me neither."

"Don't be surprised if he plays mind games. Don't fall for it."

Don't fall for it? I already fell for it.

"I'll try."

"I know you will." Sanford's face turned serious. "Shawn, there's something I want to talk to you about. They're talking about another mission for me."

"When?" Shawn asked cautiously.

"It's very vague. Soon, I think. But it still looks good for me to see the show." Sanford smiled strangely, and it seemed like there was something else he wanted to tell Shawn. Then he seemed to think better of it

"Shawn? Focus on today, not tomorrow or the next day."

"Okay."

"Good. You're going to do . . . hold on a sec."

Shawn saw his father turn; someone was talking to him. Then the webcam went black for a couple of nerve-racking seconds before his father came back into view.

"I've got to go back on duty. Let me know how things shape up for the second round."

"If I get that far," Shawn commented.

"*When* you get that far," his dad corrected. "Now go do what needs to be done."

* * * *

"Welcome, members of the WWE Universe!" Michael Cole and Jerry Lawler, the announcers for *Monday Night Raw*, stood in the ring with microphones in hand. Cole wore a jacket and tie, while Lawler had on his usual T-shirt and jeans combination. Cole was acting as master of ceremonies. "Welcome to our quest for WWE's very first SuperFan! Let's meet our four finalists and their mentors!"

There was no applause. This first event would not take place in front of spectators. There was too much work underway in the Georgia Dome, getting it ready for WrestleMania on Sunday, to allow fans in the arena. As Shawn waited in the contestants' area with Spike, DeJuan, and Jayden—family and friends were seated several rows away—he'd been amazed by the hardworking army of designers, artists, and laborers. The biggest group was erecting the Superstars' entrance, with its floor-to-roof facade and pyramid of video screens, plus a walkway of interlocking gold and silver tiles. Meanwhile, fireworks crews were setting up equipment on every level of the arena.

"I think he's talking about us," DeJuan joked. "If not, we're in big trouble."

Shawn laughed. He was near DeJuan and Jayden, while three empty seats separated Jayden from Spike. Every so often, Spike caught their eyes and flexed his huge biceps. Then he'd wave at them as if to say, "Bye-bye! It's already over!"

All the contenders were dressed in identical warm-up outfits and running shoes, but each sported a different colored shirt. Shawn's was yellow. Spike—who had been assigned a black jersey—had some choice words when he saw Shawn's outfit: "Weenie yellow for a weenie!"

"Mentors, please join me in the ring!" Cole made the announcement. Rey, CM Punk, The Miz, and Natalya, all dressed to wrestle, climbed into the ring. Rey was wearing maroon pants and a matching mask. Shawn saw Rey stare daggers at Punk, who returned the scowl.

"What do you guys think of Spike?" DeJuan whispered to Shawn and Jayden.

Shawn made a face. Jayden did the same. "He's so annoying," she mouthed.

"And now, our four SuperFan finalists! Spike Murcer! DeJuan Smith! Jayden Starr! Shawn Reynolds!"

Spike broke ahead of the other three and did a Punk-style running slide between the ring apron and bottom rope that drew cheers from nearby workmen. Shawn entered the ring more carefully, using the metal steps.

"It's the next SuperFan!" Rey greeted him with a warm embrace.

"I hope so."

"I know so. Get yourself ready."

Shawn unzipped his warm-ups and handed them to Rey. He looked across the ring at Natalya and Jayden. Natalya had dressed to match Jayden's pink top, with pink leggings and a pink and white halter top adorned with silver sparkles. She'd even added a pink streak to her long blond hair.

Rey dropped to one knee near Shawn. "I have only one question for you, Shawn. Are you as ready as you could possibly be?"

Shawn thought for a moment. He was stronger than ever. He was a better reader. And he'd done it all without his father being home to support him.

"Yes."

"Then you'll do your best. Know how easy it is for me to bodyslam Big Show?"

"How easy?" Big Show was seven feet tall and weighed over four hundred pounds.

Rey shook his head. "Almost impossible! But I still give it my best shot."

The ringside bell got everyone's attention. Since the first competition was being taped for streaming on the WWE website, Cole gave a brief recap with emphasis on the winner's future college scholarship. Then Shawn finally learned what would happen today.

"You'll be running an obstacle course that will test your speed, your strength, your endurance, and your balance. You'll run, you'll climb stairs, you'll crawl on your belly under a rope lattice, you'll carry dumbbells from place to place, and you'll finish by circling this ring ten times and then blasting through a set of tackling dummies. Watch out for surprises!"

"Your mentors cannot help you. When you get past the tackling dummies, run to the center of the ring and sound this bell." Jerry Lawler struck an oversize bell. The sound reverberated through the Dome.

"The last competitor to finish will be eliminated. In case of a dispute, my decision will be final. Mentors ready?" Cole asked.

The mentors raised their hands.

"Contestants ready?"

Shawn raised his hand. So did the other three kids. Jerry Lawler led the four contenders to a starting gate that had been erected near the Superstars' entrance. A bright white guiding light illuminated the hundred-yard straightaway that would start the course, which then veered upward into the seats.

Michael Cole stood by the gate with his microphone. "SuperFan finalists, take your marks, get set . . . go!"

The gate dropped. The race was on.

It didn't take more than twenty yards for Shawn to find himself squarely in last place.

CHAPTER FOURTEEN

Three-quarters of the way through the race, Shawn was still dead last.

He'd sprinted gamely. Shimmied under the ropes. Moved a stack of ten-pound weight-lifting plates from one area to another. Climbed up stairs. Climbed down stairs. Yet the other competitors continued to pull away. By the time he reached the ring, Spike and Jayden had already sounded the big bell, and DeJuan was one lap from finishing. The only reason he wasn't done was that he'd gotten his feet hopelessly tangled in the ropes course.

"Come on, Shawn! Run!" He could hear his brother and Alex. What was the use? It was over, but Shawn tried to speed up, anyway.

He couldn't explain what happened next. Afterward, neither could DeJuan.

Maybe DeJuan had started celebrating a bit too early. Maybe he lost concentration. Or maybe he just hit a slick spot on the floor.

Whatever it was, DeJuan's right foot slipped out

from under him. Down he went. Shawn saw him try to break his fall with his hands. This was a huge mistake; DeJuan landed squarely on both wrists as Shawn passed him.

"Yeow!" DeJuan shouted with pain. Paramedics rushed to him. Shawn stopped and turned back, wanting to help his new friend.

"Keep going!" Rey shouted.

"Don't stop!" Alex and Peter called together. "Go, Shawn! Go!"

Shawn didn't listen. He stayed with DeJuan. It felt wrong to finish the race if DeJuan couldn't get up.

It took DeJuan himself to get Shawn moving, speaking through obvious discomfort. "Shawn! Run, dude! I can't do this competition now. My wrists are messed up! You want Spike to go one-on-one with Jayden? Finish the race!"

That did it. Shawn ran. He finished his ten laps, went to the bell, and rang it loudly.

"And our third SuperFan finalist is Shawn Reynolds from Columbia, Missouri!" Michael Cole made the announcement.

Shawn had gotten through. But as he looked at DeJuan, who was now getting his wrists splinted, he knew it had only happened because he got lucky. Or, because DeJuan got unlucky.

Which is exactly what Spike said to him on their way out of the ring. Actually, what he said was, "You lucked out, Weenie."

✳ ✳ ✳ ✳

"You think you lucked out," Rey said flatly.

"I don't *think* so. I know so. If DeJuan hadn't wiped out, he'd be in and I'd be gone." Shawn shook his head at the unfairness of it all.

Rey shook his own head right back at Shawn. "And if the sun hadn't come up this morning, we'd be in the dark. The only thing you can do is keep going. Like at SummerSlam, against Kane? He was killing me. But I just kept going."

It was three hours later. Shawn had eaten a quiet lunch in the hotel suite. Now, he and Rey were out for a walk in Atlanta's Centennial Olympic Park. Built for the 1996 Atlanta Olympic Games, it featured a huge fountain with hundreds of jets, paths with bricks engraved with the names of Olympics donors, and a replica of the Olympics torch. The park was full of tourists and office workers taking a break to enjoy the spring sunshine. Just like last night, Rey wore jeans and a leather jacket, plus one of his masks. Shawn noticed a lot of people whispering and smiling as they recognized the famous Superstar.

Shawn stopped. "Umm . . . there's only one problem with what you're saying."

"What's that?" Rey stopped, too.

"At SummerSlam? Kane beat you."

For a moment, Rey looked dumbfounded. Then he tilted his head back and laughed heartily. "Nice work with your playbook. So true, so true. But that doesn't mean I didn't keep going." There were several wooden benches near the fountain; Rey sat and motioned for Shawn to join him.

"Here's the thing, Shawn," Rey said. "You can go through life and go through life and no one notices you. Then you earn the right to be noticed. It may sound crazy, but I had to earn the right to wear this mask. Not from another person. From myself."

Shawn stretched out his hamstrings as Rey had taught him. His legs were tight from the morning's race. "How did you know you were ready to wear the mask?"

"I did hundreds of 619s before I hit it right. Hundreds of hurricanranas. Frog splashes. Flying spinning kicks, flying neckbreakers, flying back elbows, powerbombs, missile dropkicks, and planchas. You know what? Even when a professional misses those moves it hurts. You talked about Kane beating me at SummerSlam. Did I quit? No. It cuts the other way, too, amigo. When I got lucky in the Royal Rumble, did I get all mopey and dopey? Did I say, 'Hey, man, I don't deserve this, please take my championship'?"

Shawn was silent. He knew the answer: No.

"Neither will you. But sometimes a competitor needs a little short-term incentive." Rey smiled mysteriously.

What could be a better incentive than being SuperFan?

"This is what I mean." Rey reached in his back pocket, took out a folded piece of leather cloth, and handed it to Shawn. As Shawn opened it, his eyes grew wide. It was a Rey Mysterio–style wrestling mask. Silver and black, with the SuperFan logo across the top, flanked by two tornados. The difference was, this mask had the initials *S R* on each cheek. For Shawn Reynolds.

"Wow."

"You like it?"

Shawn nodded without taking his eyes off the mask. "I love it."

"Good. Just like mine, it's in the tradition of *lucha libre* from Mexico. Now give it back." Rey put his hand out. "You don't get to wear it until the final event. Incentive."

Shawn reluctantly handed over the mask. Rey wouldn't even let him try it on. But his mentor was right. He was already picturing himself in the finals, wearing this mask, competing with Spike. He was sure it would be Spike, too. How would Spike feel if he saw Shawn in this mask?

He'll probably call me Weenie Mask Boy, Shawn realized. *But it would freak him out.*

"I'm going to get to wear this," Shawn promised his mentor.

Rey laughed and draped an arm around Shawn's shoulder. "You'd better. It's not exactly recyclable. Come on, you've got your community service tonight. Let's head back."

CHAPTER FIFTEEN

The sleek guitar felt great in Shawn's hands. It was a Takamine acoustic, much better than the cheap one he had at home. But Shawn hadn't given it a moment's attention since they'd moved into the suite on Thursday night. Now, playing it seemed like the perfect way to chill before the community service hospital visit.

He unconsciously started picking out the notes to Rey Mysterio's theme song, "Booyaka 619," but gave it a twist of his own, adding a riff here, jazzing it up there.

A gentle tap at the door interrupted Shawn's playing.

"Come in!" Shawn called.

"You sound great," his mom declared as she stepped inside. Then her voice turned gentle. "Maybe you can play that again for me?"

"I don't think so. Thanks," Shawn said sheepishly.

"Not to worry," his mother assured him. "How

was the walk with Rey? Helpful?"

Shawn nodded. "Very. He made a mask for me. I can only wear it if I get through this next challenge."

Carla chuckled. "Incentive, huh?"

"That's what Rey said!" Shawn exclaimed.

Carla nodded knowingly. "All adults think alike." She hesitated. "I don't want to sound all sappy here. But I wonder sometimes if grown-ups emphasize all the wrong things. To get good grades, to make lots of money. When the most important thing of all is what you already are, Shawn. I saw it when you stopped to help your friend in that race. A good person." Carla's eyes twinkled. "Mask or no mask."

"Thanks, Mom." Shawn meant it. "Any news from Dad today?"

There was a strange look in his mom's eyes. "Nothing to report."

"I think I'll send him another e-mail."

Carla smiled. "No matter where he is when he reads it, I think he'd like that very, very much."

★ ★ ★ ★

WELCOME, SUPERFANS! YAY SHAWN! YAY JAYDEN!

A hand-lettered banner greeted Shawn and Jayden when they stepped out of the elevator onto the pediatrics floor of the Atlanta Peachtree Hospital. Then the banner was somehow cut loose and fell to the ground. Behind it was a cheering group of fifteen kids of all ages. Some stood with IV poles, others were on crutches or in wheelchairs. "We love you guys! Welcome to peeds!"

Shawn and Jayden looked at each other, not really sure what to do.

The two of them, plus their families, had been shuttled from the hotel to the hospital by minivan. DeJuan was visiting a senior center, and Spike was at the zoo, which Shawn felt was sort of appropriate.

The cheering continued until a boy around Peter's age rolled forward in a motorized wheelchair. He was very thin, African American, and had close-cropped hair. "I'm Taylor Swett, and I'm the prez of this floor."

Since when does a hospital ward have a president?

"I'm prez because I'm here the most and the longest." Taylor was beaming. "I've got juvenile rheumatoid arthritis. You don't want it. I'm here for hand surgery. I had foot surgery a few weeks ago. That's why I'm in a wheelchair. Check out my digits!"

Taylor lifted his right hand. Shawn could see the middle and ring finger knuckles were badly swollen. "Everyone here loves you guys. We hate that Spike dude."

"Spike stinks!" one of the kids shouted to much laughter.

"Follow the rolling wheelchair, SuperFans! We've got a party planned in the lounge." Taylor expertly spun his wheelchair around, and everyone followed him toward the lounge.

The lounge had been decked out in WWE gear. There was juice and chips, and the patients put on a show for the guests of honor. Accompanied on guitar by a goateed male nurse named Clarence, they sang the arena entrance songs of various Superstars. Then Taylor played *Wii Raw vs. SmackDown* against a *Latina* girl named Mariah. Mariah insisted that Jayden be her assistant; Taylor got Shawn to coach him. Mariah won easily. The party finished up with an autograph session. Jayden and Shawn found it amazing that their signatures could be so meaningful.

When Clarence announced that it was time to wrap up, the kids booed but complied. Mariah hung back and then asked Jayden if she would sign a poster in her room. Jayden said she'd be thrilled to, and she took her family along. That left Shawn and his group alone with Taylor.

"Shawn, how about we meet you by the elevator?" Carla asked.

"Sounds good. I'll come . . . soon."

Carla moved off, leaving the two boys alone. For the first time that evening, Taylor seemed shy. Shawn knew he should take the lead.

"Are you going to get to see WrestleMania?" he asked.

Taylor nodded. "I think so. On TV. If my operation isn't on Sunday."

"I wish you could be at the Dome," Shawn told him sincerely.

"I wish I could, too." Taylor's voice was sad. "I like Jayden, but I'm rooting for you."

A crazy idea was forming in Shawn's head. Maybe, just maybe . . .

"Why can't you come? I mean, if you can get a ticket, and if you haven't had your surgery?"

"They won't let me out. This isn't my first operation."

"How many have you had?"

Taylor started ticking off numbers on his fingers.

"One, two, three . . . I think this is number eight. This year."

Eight operations this year? How—

Taylor laughed. "I'm kidding! Not eight this year. Eight in all."

"Oh."

What would that be like? Eight operations? Here I am worried about the competition. Compared to what Taylor's going through? That's nothing.

There was silence again. Shawn knew that he ought to rejoin his family, but he also realized that Taylor, in some way, needed him there. Just for something to do, he got the acoustic guitar that Clarence had played and plucked idly at the strings.

"You play?" Taylor asked.

"Do I what?"

"You play? The guitar?"

"A little," Shawn admitted. "But not—"

He was about to say, "But not in front of other people," but Taylor interrupted.

"Play me something."

Shawn froze, feeling the too-familiar knot in his stomach.

"Come on, Shawn," Taylor cajoled. "I want to hear you. I bet you're good."

"I'm not good," Shawn told him.

Taylor faked playing an air guitar. "Well, I can't play at all because of my joints. So you're better than me."

I can't play at all because of my joints.

Shawn sat and strapped on Clarence's guitar. Taylor couldn't play even if he wanted to. Shawn could play. All he had to do was want to. Though sweat dripped from his armpits, Shawn started the version of "Booyaka 619" he'd created in the hotel suite. Taylor broke into a broad smile when he recognized the riff.

"Six-one-nine! Keep going!"

Shawn kept going. He added new notes as Taylor bopped happily along.

It was the weirdest thing. He couldn't pinpoint the moment, but the moment definitely happened. At some point, playing for Taylor stopped being scary. And when it stopped being scary? It started being fun.

CHAPTER SIXTEEN

Shawn came home from the hospital to a voice mail from Rey.

"Shawn, this is Rey. When's the last time you looked at *Tom Sawyer*? I don't know if you're gonna need it tomorrow, but you're gonna need it eventually. Prepare, my man."

That was enough for Shawn to set his alarm an hour early, shower quickly, eat a breakfast of instant oatmeal, and settle down with the book to test himself. What was Tom's aunt's name? Polly. Who did Tom fight to impress Becky? Henry. How did the book end, exactly?

Yikes. Shawn realized he didn't know. Not exactly. So he turned to the very last page and read carefully.

CONCLUSION.

So endeth this chronicle. It being strictly a history of a BOY, it must stop here; the story could not go much further without becoming the history of a MAN. When one writes a novel about grown people, he knows exactly where to stop—that is, with a marriage; but when he writes of juveniles, he must stop where he best can.

Most of the characters that perform in this book still live, and are prosperous and happy. Some day it may seem worth while to take up the story of the younger ones again and see what sort of men and women they turned out to be; therefore it will be wisest not to reveal any of that part of their lives at present.

THE END.

Huh. That's not what he thought. He thought it had ended with Tom and Huckleberry Finn talking about forming a gang of robbers, since robbers were so much cooler than pirates.

Well, now he knew. If the question came up, he was ready.

✳ ✳ ✳ ✳

"Can you draw at all?" Jayden asked Shawn.

"I'm decent," Shawn admitted.

"Me too. If we can get through the first part, I think we can send Spike home." Jayden's eyes shone at the possibility.

"So do I." Shawn looked over at Spike, who was discussing strategy with his father and CM Punk. It was more than discussion. Spike's father was right in his son's face. "He deserves to lose. Look what I found outside my hotel door."

Shawn dug out a folded sheet of newsprint. It was a faked front page of a newspaper. The two-word headline was gigantic: WEENIE LOSER!!! Under it was an Internet photograph of Shawn.

Jayden smiled grimly. "I got you beat." She reached into her jacket pocket for a similar sheet of newsprint. Hers read: WWE STUPID-FAN!!! Under it was a photograph of Jayden.

"How can we be sure that Spike did those?" Shawn wondered. Then he and Jayden cracked up. If it hadn't been Spike, then who? DeJuan?

It was almost ten o'clock on Saturday morning, the start of the second SuperFan challenge. Once again, the Georgia Dome was free of spectators except for the contestants' families, but there were twice as many workers as the day before, since WrestleMania was only twenty-nine hours away. Once again, the challenge would be taped for streaming on the WWE website.

Shawn had an odd feeling. He felt confident. The competition would be in two parts. They'd start in the ring, where special hydraulics had been installed that would bounce the ring like a trampoline. Each contestant had to keep his or her balance for sixty seconds. Then he or she had to make their way to an assortment of poster board and art supplies at ringside. In five minutes, that competitor had to create a WWE-themed poster. No do-overs, either. You got points for how steady you were in the ring and points for how good your one poster turned out.

"Hey, you two." DeJuan, dressed in jeans and a T-shirt with both wrists splinted, came over to say hello.

"How are you feeling?" Shawn asked.

"Like I shouldn't have wiped out yesterday," DeJuan replied. "Also, hating Spike." He leaned in close. "I found this on my doorstep this morning." He unfolded a newspaper page much like the ones Shawn and Jayden had found. The headline read: BYE-BYE DEJUAN!

"We got the same thing," Jayden told him.

"I practically caught him planting mine." DeJuan snorted. "I heard noise outside my suite. When I opened the door, he was right there. Of course, he denied everything."

Shawn looked over at Spike again. His father was still in his face. In fact, Mr. Murcer was yelling so loudly that it was impossible not to overhear.

"You lose today, Spike, and you're gonna lose TV for a year. I'm going to ground you for the rest of your life. Don't lose. You understand me? Do not lose!" Mr. Murcer glared at his son.

"Yes, sir," Spike answered quietly.

"Are you wimping out on me, loser? I can't hear you!"

"Yes, sir!"

Shawn winced. His own father would never talk to him like that. He felt bad for Spike. Very bad, in fact.

Just then, the big bell sounded, calling the contestants to the ring. Michael Cole and Jerry Lawler were again doing the announcing and judging.

"Fifteen minutes from now," Cole intoned with gravity, "the WWE Universe will know the identities of our two SuperFan finalists. Those two will return at four this afternoon, in front of a live audience, to determine our very first SuperFan! Clear the ring except for the contestants, please."

A male voice rang out from ringside, sharp and scary. "Kill 'em, Spike!"

Spike's father. Shawn and Jayden shared a doubtful look as they stood near each other in the ring with Spike by the far corner. *Kill 'em?* Wasn't that a little bit extreme?

Without any warning, or even a bell sounding, the ring started to bounce crazily. All three kids were caught by surprise. A split-second later, Shawn found himself on his butt. He bounced to his feet as Rey called encouragement. "Balance, Shawn. Balance! Just like on the stadium bleachers!"

Even though Shawn lost his footing several times, he didn't panic because the same thing was happening to Spike and Jayden. In fact, Spike was having the hardest time with it as Punk and his father bellowed useless instructions. Spike kept wiping out. Shawn, meanwhile, found that if he let his knees absorb the shock, he could maintain his footing. Jayden discovered the same trick.

Spike didn't.

Michael Cole called the action. "Shawn is almost there. Five seconds left for Shawn! Ten seconds left for Jayden! Spike goes down again! Shawn's done! Go do your poster, Shawn! Jayden, five seconds. Three, two, one, go!"

Shawn and Jayden's cheering sections hollered as the two friends got to work. Shawn knew what he was going to make: a WrestleMania poster featuring a mask like the one Rey had promised him for the finals. He started sketching and then glanced to his right, where Jayden was drawing happily with a glitter marker and fast-drying red paint.

"Spike's going down!" she called with glee as Spike finally got the go-ahead to start on his poster.

"I know!" Shawn did the lettering, then filled in the mask.

"Looking good, Picasso," Rey commented. Shawn had been concentrating so hard that he hadn't even noticed his mentor behind him. "Looking great!"

"One minute, Shawn! One minute, ten seconds, Jayden. Four minutes, Spike!"

Jerry Lawler announced the update. Shawn didn't even need the whole minute. A bit of gold paint on the mask, and he was done with thirty seconds to spare. He marched his poster to Cole and Lawler. Then he ran over to his rooting section. His brother and Alex pounded him happily on the back and his mother beamed.

"You did great!" Alex was psyched. "You're going through for sure!"

"What a surprise!" Michael Cole shouted, getting their attention. "He can't possibly be finished. But here comes Spike!"

Here comes Spike? How was that possible?

However it was possible, it was happening, even though Spike had only been working for less than a minute. Yet Spike was trotting confidently past Jayden, who was still hard at—

"Hey! Watch it! Spike! You jerk!"

Jayden howled. Then she leaped to her feet and pointed an accusing finger at Spike, who was still making his way toward Cole and Lawler. "He ruined my poster! He ruined my poster!"

Jayden was close to tears. Shawn dashed over to Jayden and saw what had happened: A huge container of black paint had somehow spilled, obliterating her artwork. Meanwhile, Spike was handing his own poster—a sloppy sign that read "WrestleMania XXVII" to the two MCs.

"He ruined my poster!" Jayden shouted again.

"No, I didn't!" Spike defended himself as Peter came running out of the audience.

"I saw everything!" Peter yelled. Shawn had never seen his brother so angry. "You kicked paint on her poster."

"Get outta here, squirt!" Spike demanded. "Whoever you are!"

"I'm Shawn's brother, and I saw you cheat. Cheater! Cheater!" Peter turned to Michael Cole. "I saw Spike cheat. Kick him out!"

"Yeah!" Spike scoffed. "Like you're not doing this because of your brother!"

A huge argument ensued. Natalya jumped in on Jayden's behalf. So did Rey. For a solid minute, they argued with Cole. Meanwhile, Spike moved to stand with his father and CM Punk, and all of them tried to suppress big grins.

At first, Cole claimed that there was nothing he could do, since he hadn't seen Spike do anything wrong.

"Look at the videotape!" Natalya insisted.

Cole agreed to check the tape. However, it turned out that the cameraman closest to Jayden had a malfunctioning camera. The video was pure snow. Absolutely useless. When Jayden heard this, she howled again. "But Shawn's brother saw everything!"

"Listen to her! I saw everything!" Peter pushed toward Michael Cole.

That's when CM Punk stepped between Peter and the MC. There was no visual proof. Peter was biased. Jayden could have dumped paint on her own poster because it wasn't any good. Spike turned in a poster, while Jayden never did. Bottom line: Cole needed to declare Spike the second finalist.

Cole and Jerry Lawler conferred. Then Cole stepped forward.

"The winner of the second SuperFan challenge: Shawn Reynolds of Columbia, Missouri. The runner-up, joining Shawn in the Ultimate SuperFan Challenge today at four o'clock . . . Spike Murcer!"

Shawn looked at Jayden. She was bawling in Natalya's arms. He glanced at Spike, again with his father and CM Punk. They were laughing. "Good job," Shawn heard Spike's father exclaim. "It's not how you play the game, it's whether you win or lose!"

Shawn's eyes narrowed to angry slits. He felt bad that Spike had a father with an attitude like that. But he felt worse that Jayden had been cheated.

His brother edged up to him. "Shawn, you've gotta take this cheater. You have to."

Shawn swallowed hard. His brother was right. He had to beat Spike in the final.

But how? The guy would do absolutely anything to win.

CHAPTER SEVENTEEN

Hi, Shawn!

You are really cute, and in about five years I hope that you will be my boyfriend.

Alicia

Shawn,

I am so angry for Jayden. I know there is no proof that Spike ruined her poster, but that doesn't mean he didn't do it P.S. I read *Tom Sawyer,* too.

Jose

The WWE had set up a place on its website where fans could send positive e-mails to the competitors. Just after lunch, Shawn sat at the suite's computer, flanked by Jayden and Peter to his left and DeJuan and Alex to his right. While the grown-ups ate in the dining room, the kids checked out some of the hundreds of e-mails.

"Want to answer Jose?" Shawn asked Jayden.

"He wrote to you. You do it," she suggested.

"Tell him you think that Jayden got ripped off!" Alex urged. "And that you're going to rip Spike—"

"Got it." Shawn turned his attention to the keyboard.

Jose,

Like my friend Alex says, I think Jayden got ripped off. I talked to Rey, and he said the best thing I could do would be to beat Spike fair and square. I will never cheat the way that Spike did. That's not winning. Thank you for being my fan.

Shawn Reynolds

He typed his last name and looked back at his friends. "How's that?"

Alex rolled his eyes. "I think you're too nice."

"Alex is right. Spike could do it again. What if he does?" Peter asked.

"I don't know." Shawn pushed back from the keyboard.

Jayden slapped her hands on her thighs. "I should have expected him to try something. I think you need to plan, Shawn."

"Plan?" Shawn was frustrated. "How? I don't even know what the last event is going to be!"

"Well, you know some things," DeJuan corrected. "You gotta figure that the book is going to be involved."

"And you know the crowd is going to be rooting

for you," Jayden said.

Jayden was right. Shawn probably would have the audience behind him. How big an audience there'd be, he wasn't sure. The WWE offered free tickets to several thousand young fans. The thought of all those people watching him made Shawn wince. Yes, he'd played his guitar for Taylor at the hospital. But that was an audience of one. Shawn remembered the nightmare on the plane and his non-speech at the assembly. Would he freeze up, unable to move or think? And what if Spike *did* cheat? Wasn't the smart thing to do to cheat right back?

Shawn didn't know the answer to any of these questions. Not a single one.

✶ ✶ ✶ ✶

"Shawn!" His mother called from the living room. "E-mail from your dad!"

Shawn put down *Tom Sawyer*—he'd been reviewing it one more time——and hustled back out to the computer nook.

"I'm afraid you're going to be disappointed," Carla told him. "Read."

With a sick feeling worse than stage fright, Shawn leaned toward the monitor.

My dear family,

I love you all.

You know the army. When you are asked to go on a mission, you don't say no. The army has asked me to go on a special mission. I will be traveling alone. In fact, by the time you read this, the mission will be underway. As a result of this mission, I will be unable to watch WrestleMania at my base. I'll find out the results just as soon as I can. I mean it. I'll do anything to find out. Shawn, I hope you are not too disappointed by this. I wish you the best of luck. Again, I could not be prouder of you if you were my own son. Hey! You *are* my own son! Carla and Peter, I love you both. See you all before you know it. I'm right beneath you.

Dad

"You okay?" Carla asked.

Shawn nodded, though he felt shaken. "I guess. I just feel bad for Dad. Does Peter know?"

Carla shook her head. "Not yet. I'll tell him. Shawn? Your father is coming home. Don't worry. He's coming home."

Carla spoke with conviction. There was something convincing in his mother's tone. This was Sanford Reynolds they were talking about. He was a highly trained soldier. He'd be okay.

"You go get ready," his mom instructed. "I understand there's a little competition this afternoon that one of my kids is part of."

Shawn pumped his fist in the air as he started down the hallway, trying to show his mother confidence he didn't quite feel.

★ ★ ★ ★

There were enough kids milling around outside the Dome to make Shawn's stomach do a loop-the-loop.

While his family and Alex were taken to a VIP seating area, Rodrigo escorted Shawn to his own locker room to dress and prepare for the finals. His new outfit was gold: gold shorts, a gold and black top, and gold and black running shoes. All good. But one part of his competition outfit was missing. His mask.

"Will I see Rey before I go up?" Shawn asked.

Rodrigo nodded. "Absolutely. He says he's got something for you."

Shawn smiled happily. Rey hadn't forgotten!

Rodrigo stepped out to make a phone call, and Shawn went to the three-quarter-length mirror near the showers to check out his outfit from every angle. He loved how his first name was spelled out in block letters across the rear of his shirt: *S-H-A-W-N*.

"Hey! They've got the wrong name! It should say *W-E-E-N-I-E!*"

Oh no. Spike. Somehow he'd gotten into the locker room.

Spike marched over and got in Shawn's face. His all-black outfit looked scary. "I've got a great idea, Weenie. Why don't we settle this SuperFan thing before we even go upstairs? You and me. One fall. Loser leaves town. Right here, right now!"

CHAPTER EIGHTEEN

"Right here," Spike repeated. "Right now. Loser leaves town. One fall. You in, Weenie?"

Shawn took a quick look around, hoping that someone—anyone!—would come to his rescue. There was no one. He knew that even if he didn't agree to Spike's ridiculous suggestion that they wrestle "right here, right now. Loser leaves town," Spike could hurt him in a way that would render the finals meaningless.

How had the WWE let this guy into the competition, anyway?

"You in, Weenie? Right here, right now? Loser leaves town?"

"I think you need to have someone else write your lines," Shawn fired back courageously. "You keep repeating yourself."

Maybe it was the wrong approach, making Spike mad, but Shawn was glad that he was finally standing up for himself. Then he thought about what he had seen that morning, with Spike being chewed out by his own father. How much of Spike was Spike, and how much was a reaction to a father who would treat him that way?

Shawn decided to find out. Gently.

"You know, Spike. I think you're a great competitor."

"I'm *the* great competitor. You're the weenie."

Spike was obviously not flattered. Shawn pressed on, though. "You're in the finals. You must be under a lot of . . . a lot of pressure."

"What do you mean?"

"Well, I saw you with your father. He really wants you to win. I don't know if that makes it easier or harder."

"Well," Spike mimicked, "it's a lot more than I can say for your dad. He didn't even bother to come!"

Shawn exploded with fury. No one busted on his dad and got away with it. "That's because he's over in Afghanistan!"

Spike was silent. Thoughtful even. "I didn't know."

"You didn't know?" Shawn asked, marginally less angry. "Come on. You had to know! It was all over my video."

"My dad wouldn't let me watch. He wanted me to be focused and promote myself." Shawn rubbed his chin. "Your dad's in Afghanistan, huh? That's gotta be rough."

It was almost like Spike was being human. Almost. Then his opponent hardened.

"Well, Weenie, it's been nice chatting and all that. But my dad's gonna lose his cookies if I don't win, and I don't wanna be around for that. Ready to go, right now? Let's do it!"

Spike made a quick move toward Shawn, and Shawn put up his hands. He couldn't fight Spike off, but maybe he could buy some time. Just as Shawn felt Spike's fingers lock on his shoulders, a deep adult voice boomed.

"Spike Murcer! What are you doing?"

It was Rey.

Spike whirled, all innocence. "I was just wishing Shawn good luck."

In five quick strides, Rey joined them. He wore a wrestling outfit in the same colors as Shawn's competition clothes, plus a mask. "Spike Murcer, I don't believe it for a minute. Get your sorry self out of my face. Go!"

There was no hesitation. Spike turned and ran out of the locker room.

"What was that about?" Rey demanded.

"He wanted to wrestle me right here for the title."

Rey shook his head sadly. "It's because of that loco father of his."

"You saw them this morning?"

"Everyone saw. And heard. I feel for the kid, I really do." Then Rey smiled. "But not so much that I don't want you to win. How do you feel?"

Shawn stepped out from between the mirrors. "Scared."

"Scared?" Rey scoffed. "Of Spike? Spike should be scared of you!"

"There are all those kids out there! And people are watching on television!" Shawn slumped on one of the locker room benches.

Rey nodded knowingly. "Ah. I got it. Stage fright. Why didn't you say something?"

"I didn't want you to think I was a weenie." Shawn could barely look at Rey.

"Come on." Rey helped Shawn up. "And no, I haven't forgotten about your mask."

Together, they left the locker room and took an escalator to the main level of the arena. The closer they came to the Superstars' entrance, the easier it was to hear the buzz of the crowd.

"That sound make you nervous?" Rey asked.

"Um . . . yes. Why are you doing this? It makes me want to barf!" If Spike had shown up right then and asked him to wrestle for the SuperFan title, Shawn would have thrown himself down and tapped out.

"That's the idea." Rey's voice was grim. "Feel sick."

What? Feel sick? Why does Rey want me to feel sick?

"I know what you're feeling. You've got all these hopes riding on you. You feel sure you can't be as good as people want you to be. You get stage fright? Fine, Shawn. Feel it! It's not gonna kill you! Feel it!!" Rey was practically shouting now.

"I am feeling it!" Shawn yelled.

"Feel it more!"

"I can't feel it more!"

"It's not gonna kill you," Rey pressed. "Feel it more!"

"I can't!"

"Good," Rey said softly. "Now feel it less."

It was the strangest thing. Shawn had heard all kinds of things about stage fright. How he should picture his audience in their underwear. How he should go to a happy place in his mind. How he should pretend he was dreaming. None of it worked. None of it, that is, until Rey Mysterio told him not to fight it, but to feel it.

Rey looked at him closely. "How you doing?"

"I'm . . . better." Shawn looked up at his mentor with thanks in his eyes.

"Good. Then put this on. Wait. Let me do it." Rey found Shawn's mask in his pocket and positioned it on Shawn's head. "You look awesome, my man. I can't wait for them to see you."

He was straightening his mask when Spike and Punk reached them.

"Nice mask, Weenie. Too ugly to be seen in public?" Spike was his usual charming self.

Shawn smiled. He was not going to get psyched out.

"Boys and girls of Atlanta: Are you ready for the Ultimate SuperFan Challenge?"

The crowd cheered the public address by the announcer.

Finally, the moment had come. Shawn didn't know whether he'd win or lose, but he knew he'd do the very best he could. Without cheating. And hopefully without stage fright.

Would that be enough to take him to victory? He'd find out very, very soon.

CHAPTER NINETEEN

As soon as the crowd saw Shawn in the mask that Rey had given him, they started chanting. "Shawn, Shawn, Shawn, Shawn!"

"Show them you hear 'em," Rey advised. "They want your love."

Shawn waved to the crowd all the way to the ring. He saw his family and Alex sitting with Jayden and DeJuan and their families. All were on their feet cheering. Peter was standing on his chair.

Just before Shawn climbed in the ring, he thought of Taylor and the other kids at the hospital watching on streaming video. He turned to the nearest TV camera, mouthed "Hi, Taylor!" and gave a little wave.

In the ring, Rey and Shawn were directed to one corner. Spike and CM Punk went to the other. Spike's father was already shouting rude instructions at his son from ringside.

Mr. McMahon himself handled the announcing duties for the finale. "Welcome to the Ultimate

SuperFan Challenge! We have two worthy competitors on hand. One will be our winner. The other, the runner-up, who will step into the role of SuperFan if the winner should be unable to continue for any reason. And now, let's welcome a very special guest!"

The Superstars' entrance lit up and the audience roared as "The Time Is Now" played. Then John Cena, wearing street clothes but carrying the championship and a mic, ran through the smoke and planted himself in the entryway. After a prolonged ovation, he climbed in the ring.

"I'll keep this short and sweet," Cena announced. "Just like I'm going to do to Sheamus tomorrow!"

The crowd erupted again. The rivalry between Sheamus and Cena had all the intensity of the feud between Rey and CM Punk.

"One of these two young men will be your SuperFan. He will earn a college scholarship. He will represent the future of the WWE Universe. And he will carry in my championship!"

Shawn stood with his hands on the ropes and swallowed hard. He felt the familiar clutch of fright at the notion that he might enter this Dome tomorrow with Cena.

"Feel it," he muttered to himself. "Feel it."

Cena stepped away so Mr. McMahon could explain the rules for the final event. The first part would be a test of strength—a tug-of-war. Then would come a test of endurance, where each contestant would stand on a narrow platform wide enough for just one foot. The first contestant to fall would lose. The third part would be a test about *Tom Sawyer*. The tiebreaker, if needed, would be a quiz about WWE knowledge.

Shawn hoped it wouldn't get that far.

"Would the finalists and their mentors come to the center, please?"

The "Shawn, Shawn!" chant began again as the competitors and their Superstar mentors joined Cena and Mr. McMahon in the ring. Cena looked right at Spike. "I'm watching you."

"Maybe you need to watch me, instead," Punk countered.

Without any warning, Punk leaped past Cena, grabbed Rey by the shoulders, and rolled him toward the far corner. Rey was stunned by the sudden attack but countered quickly with fast forearms to Punk's chest and jaw. As Cena and Mr. McMahon ushered the boys to safety, Punk bodyslammed Rey to the mat.

Shawn felt sure that Cena and Mr. McMahon would break up the impromptu battle, but they had clearly decided to let the Superstars do their thing.

"Come on, Rey!" Shawn bellowed at his mentor. "Wrestle smart!"

Rey bounced up, climbed to the top rope, sprang off it, and came down squarely on Punk's chest. He moved in for the pin, even though there was no referee. Instead, the crowd counted. "One! Two!"

Punk kicked out. Then he flipped Rey on his stomach, grabbed Rey's ankles, and pulled. The stress on Rey's back and tender ankle was tremendous. Shawn saw how Rey was struggling.

"Tap out!" Shawn screamed, not wanting Rey to get hurt again.

But Rey didn't tap out. Not right away, anyway. He struggled to escape. But it was no use. Finally he tapped the mat, indicating that he was submitting.

Punk let go . . . and kicked Rey's bad ankle.

Rey bellowed in agony. Punk strutted away after exchanging a high-five with Spike.

Shawn rushed to help Rey. But there was nothing he could do except watch as his mentor squirmed with pain on the canvas.

CHAPTER TWENTY

The paramedics insisted on taking Rey to the hospital. Mr. McMahon allowed Shawn to accompany him as far as the Superstars' entrance.

"I know I can't be here for you," Rey told Shawn. "But my work is done. It's in your hands now. Show them what you can do!"

Shawn couldn't speak. The idea of competing without Rey in his corner was frightening.

John Cena had come down the Superstars' entrance path near Shawn and Rey. "You ready, Shawn?"

"How can I do this without Rey?" Shawn managed.

"Because Spike's going to have to do it without Punk," Cena reported. "Mr. McMahon sent him back to the hotel."

The "Shawn, Shawn!" chant started anew.

Rey smiled through his pain. "There are four thousand kids with you. Get out there, Shawn."

Knowing Punk was gone made it easier. Shawn

and Cena returned to the ring, where Spike waited with Mr. McMahon. Two WWE aides had painted a line down the middle of the ring and brought in the tug-of-war rope. Mr. McMahon explained that the first boy to pull the other over the line would win this part of the competition.

Shawn and Spike were directed to opposite sides. Shawn wrapped the rope around his waist. Spike did the same.

CLANG! The bell rang, starting the tug-of-war. Shawn felt a mighty pull as Spike leaned into the rope.

It was the moment that Shawn had been waiting for. He let go of the rope. With no resistance, Spike tumbled clumsily backward and landed on his butt. The crowd laughed uproariously.

"You win!" Shawn stepped over the center line with satisfaction. No way he could have beaten Spike Murcer in a tug-of-war, so he'd saved his strength for the next round.

Shawn heard Peter. "Smart, Shawn! Now, dust him!"

Mr. McMahon took the mic as two workers carried the narrow platforms for the next part of the competition into the ring and placed them five feet apart. "Winner of the first round, Spike Murcer! If Spike wins this next round, he will become our SuperFan! If Shawn wins, we move to round three. Contestants, ascend your platforms!"

Shawn climbed the two-foot-high platform easily and balanced on his left foot. Spike did the same.

"Spike, ready?" Mr. McMahon asked.

Spike nodded. "Ready for the Masked Weenie to lose!"

"Shawn, ready?"

Shawn readjusted his mask. "Let's go."

CLANG! The second challenge was underway. In typical WWE fashion, it wasn't nearly as simple as it seemed.

For the first few minutes, all both boys had to do was maintain their balance. That was no problem. Then the WWE upped the stakes. Workers brought in buckets of ice water and flung the water at the contestants. The first splash made Shawn sway badly. The crowd implored him to hold on. Ten minutes passed, with a fresh bucket of water every minute. Fifteen minutes, and five more buckets. What had been simple at the beginning turned very difficult.

Then it got worse. Giant fans were set up in the ring. When they switched on, Shawn and Spike were blasted with freezing gusts of wind. How much longer could Shawn hold out? A minute? Two?

"Thirty seconds," he told himself. "Start with thirty seconds. One, two . . ."

But it didn't take that long. What it took was a sneeze, caused by the wind in Spike's face. The laws of physics were against him. First came the sneeze, then his scream of dismay, and then Spike fell from his platform.

The place went crazy.

"Shawn, Shawn, Shawn!" The chant started again.

As the boys were ushered into a private area to dry off and change, and the water was squeegeed off the canvas, Mr. McMahon talked to the crowd. "Boys and girls and WWE Universe at home," Mr. McMahon announced. "Congratulations to Shawn Reynolds, winner of our second round! Congrats to these two great competitors!"

When Shawn and Spike reemerged, two stools were already in the ring. Shawn sat in the one to the left, facing his family.

Cena took over the announcing duties. "The WWE is committed to helping kids become great readers. That's because readers are leaders. Each of our contestants was asked to read Mark Twain's novel, *The Adventures of Tom Sawyer*. For this last, deciding section of the competition, we'll test their knowledge. And asking the questions? You know him from *SmackDown* and *NXT*. He's a former Superstar, a former high school teacher, and one of our favorite broadcasters: Matt Striker!"

Shawn had seen Striker on *SmackDown*; the announcer climbed into the ring wearing a gray suit, white shirt, and maroon tie, all over a hugely muscular build. He took the mic, shook Mr. McMahon's hand, and then spoke to the competitors with the authoritative voice of a former teacher.

"Shawn and Spike, the rules are simple. It's sudden death. Get the question right? Go on. Get it wrong? Go home."

Shawn felt ready. No way could Spike know *Tom Sawyer* better than he did.

Very quickly, Shawn found out that he was wrong.

CHAPTER TWENTY-ONE

CLANG! The deciding part of the Ultimate SuperFan Challenge was underway.

Striker started with Spike. "Spike, first question. What is the name of Tom Sawyer's younger brother?"

"Sid!"

"That is correct." Striker stepped toward Shawn. "Shawn, when Tom and his friends run away from home to fake their own deaths, what is the name of the island where they hide?"

"Jackson's Island!" Shawn answered immediately.

"That is correct. Spike, what does Tom do for the first time on that island that makes him sick to his stomach?"

"He smokes a pipe!" Spike punched the air, knowing he'd nailed it.

"Correct! Shawn, what is Tom's excuse for trying to cut school at the beginning of the novel?"

Tougher question, but Shawn knew the answer. "He says his sore toe is mortified!"

"Meaning rotting. Exactly. Good job!"

The "Shawn, Shawn!" chant started again so loudly that Striker had to ask for quiet before he posed his next question. "Spike. When Tom tricks his friends into painting the fence, what color is the paint?"

"White!"

There was a smattering of applause, since Spike had obviously done his homework.

The questions kept coming. Why are Tom and Becky in the cave? As part of a birthday party. What kind of insect does Tom play with in school? A doodlebug. What do the boys find buried in the graveyard? Gold coins.

It was Spike's turn.

"Spike, at the book's end, what do Tom and Huck decide they will do together?"

"Give me something tough, Matt," Spike said confidently. "At the end of the book, Tom and Huck decide to form a gang of robbers."

Matt nodded his head appreciatively. "Great job!" He turned back to Shawn.

"Shawn. To stay alive in this competition: How does the book end?"

Spike? I owe you one. This is going to be fun.

Shawn knew the answer, but he hesitated and

feigned panic. He glanced over at Spike, who half-grinned and half-sneered, praying for Shawn to fail.

"Do you know the answer, Shawn?" Matt asked sharply. "Or is Spike our winner?"

Shawn waited longer, making Spike and Matt believe that he was stuck.

"Three seconds, Shawn," Matt warned as the Dome fell silent.

"Oh. Oh my gosh. I'm not sure." Shawn made himself sound lost and defeated.

One more peek at Spike. His opponent could practically taste victory.

"Guess," Matt urged.

Shawn made his voice small as if anticipating defeat. "Okay. I'll take a guess. It ended with a chapter called 'Conclusion,' where Mr. Twain told the readers that he would save more of the story for later."

Striker paused and swallowed loudly into the mic. The crowd held their breaths. "Shawn Reynolds . . . that is correct!"

Shawn took another look at Spike, who was slumping on his stool, angry that Shawn had known the answer. But Shawn could detect something else there, too—was there a little respect in Spike's eyes?

"The competition is not over!" Matt reminded

the cheering crowd. "Since both SuperFan finalists are such experts on *Tom Sawyer*, we now move to a tiebreaking question about WWE history. Mr. McMahon?"

Mr. McMahon took the microphone. "I am going to ask both boys one question. The first to answer it correctly shall be our SuperFan. Shawn? Spike?"

Spike was ready. Shawn was ready. The crowd was ready.

"Spike and Shawn, everyone knows that *SmackDown* moved to the Syfy network last October. That first night on Syfy, your mentors, Rey Mysterio and CM Punk, each competed. Spike, who did Punk fight? Shawn, who did Rey fight? And what was the result?"

Shawn racked his brains. He hadn't been a WWE fan last October. In fact, he barely knew what *SmackDown* was last October. What kind of question is that? It hadn't been in his briefing notebook. How could he possibly—

Oh no. Spike knows.

Spike's hand flashed in the air.

"That first broadcast on Syfy? It took place on October 1, 2010. Punk and Rey fought each other!"

Spike's voice was triumphant.

"And who won?" Mr. McMahon prompted with a big smile on his face.

"CM Punk! Of course!"

The crowd was silent. Stunned even. After all the rooting for Shawn, it seemed like Spike had just nailed down the SuperFan crown.

Mr. McMahon smiled even more broadly. "Spike Murcer. Your answer is . . . incorrect!"

"What!? NO!!!" everyone heard Spike's father exclaim angrily. Even Mr. McMahon. He turned to the audience, found Mr. Murcer, and scowled.

"There's enough pressure on these boys! Have a little respect. Thank you."

The crowd applauded loudly.

The moment gave Shawn a chance to think. Punk and Rey hadn't fought each other. Who could Rey have fought, then? Jack Swagger? Kane? Edge? He closed his eyes. He had the thinnest memory of someone saying something to him once about that first night on Syfy. Who? Rey? His father?

His father! Yes! Way back at the *Raw* show in St. Louis!

Last October I watched Rey in this amazing match against Alberto Del Rio on the night that

SmackDown *moved over to the Syfy network. He pulled that one out. Maybe he can do it again.*

"Shawn? Any ideas?" Mr. McMahon prompted.

"I think . . . I think that Rey fought Alberto Del Rio. And he beat him."

Again, Mr. McMahon hesitated. Then . . .

"Shawn? . . . That's correct! You're our SuperFan!"

Mr. McMahon got no further. The place went wild. Fireworks, smoke, music.

Shawn had won. He had actually won!

CHAPTER TWENTY-TWO

Dear Dad,

I won! I still can't believe it. I am thinking about you every minute. Mom says that when you come home to America, we will have a big party at the house and watch all the SuperFan videos from start to finish. I want to say thank you for finding those tickets to *Raw* for Peter's birthday. If it weren't for that, I would never have entered.

There are only two things that would make this more perfect than it is. One would be if I could get my friend Taylor in the hospital a ticket to WrestleMania tomorrow. He doesn't know yet, but I'm working on that.

The other would be if you could be here, too.

Love,

Shawn

Shawn pressed send. He hoped his dad could read the e-mail soon.

CHAPTER TWENTY-THREE

"Shawn, I know you sort of met the champ yesterday, but you weren't SuperFan yesterday. Shawn, meet the champ, John Cena. Cena? Meet the first SuperFan, Shawn Reynolds. And Cena? Be glad you're not meeting me today in the ring!"

It was the next afternoon, the Sunday afternoon of WrestleMania. Shawn, Rey—mostly recovered from Punk's surprise attack from the day before, but still walking with a bit of a limp—and John Cena were together in the champions' locker room, while three floors above, Kid Rock was warming up the sold-out crowd.

As Shawn watched, Cena pulled on his famous purple jersey and tugged on his baseball cap. Later, he'd tangle with Sheamus in a special Casket Match, where victory could only come when one Superstar closed the other Superstar inside a ringside coffin. Shawn would accompany Cena to the ring and carry in his championship.

Cena shook hands with Shawn. "I couldn't say

this yesterday, but I was really hoping you would win."

"Thank you." Shawn suddenly felt shy. "I . . . I hope you win, too."

Rey puffed up his chest. "Cena and Sheamus are both just lucky my ankle is bum. I'd take them both on."

"A two-on-one handicap match?" Cena looked at Rey cockeyed. "You're good, Mysterio. But you wouldn't have a chance against me, Sheamus or no Sheamus. Right, Shawn?"

Yikes. Shawn loved John Cena. But he loved Rey even more.

Shawn waggled his head. "It depends on whether there's a quiz about *Tom Sawyer*."

The two Superstars were silent for a moment. Then they both burst out laughing.

"Nice dodge, Shawn-a-reeno," Cena sputtered. "Nice dodge."

There was loud knocking at the door.

"Come on in," Cena called.

It was Rodrigo, dressed in his black suit with his WWE credential dangling from his neck. "Hey, John and Rey. Do you have time to meet three very important friends of the SuperFan?"

The Superstars said sure—Shawn had cleared this visit beforehand—and Rodrigo opened the door wide. A moment later, an awestruck Taylor rolled into the locker room with his dad pushing the wheelchair. They were accompanied by the goateed nurse, Clarence.

"Welcome, Taylor. Welcome!" Rey and John met the visitors halfway. "I'm Rey Mysterio. This is John Cena. We're so glad you're here."

"I'm so glad I'm here, too!" Taylor exclaimed.

Shawn was psyched. The night before he'd talked by phone with Taylor's doctors. At first, they were adamant that Taylor not leave the hospital.

"How about if a nurse came with him?" Shawn asked. "To keep him safe?"

When the doctors had said that might be acceptable, Shawn called Rey. Rey phoned WWE headquarters, and three complimentary tickets and transport to the Dome were arranged. When he brought Taylor up to speed on his plan, his younger friend had nearly fainted.

As Taylor got his shirt signed by the two Superstars, Rodrigo kept an eye on the time. "Shawn, we gotta get you upstairs. Taylor, you too."

Taylor nodded. His dad thanked the Superstars.

"Hey," Rey told him. "Taylor is the real Superstar here. Go have a blast."

✳ ✳ ✳

WrestleMania XXVII.

The Georgia Dome was jammed. Shawn thought that the few thousand kids yesterday had made a lot of noise, but that was nothing compared to seventy-five thousand happy, chanting, and cheering members of the WWE Universe.

Shawn literally had the best seat in the house. He was at the announcers' table between Michael Cole and Jerry Lawler. Behind him was the SuperFan contestants' seating section, where his family and Alex were sitting with DeJuan, Jayden, and their families. Room had been made for Taylor and his group there, too. Spike and his dad had fortunately chosen to sit elsewhere.

"Welcome, members of the WWE Universe," the public address system boomed as spotlights hit the Superstars' entrance. That entrance was nothing short of amazing, and it was made even more amazing because Shawn had watched the construction work being done: forty feet high, with scores of laser lights forming a multicolored lattice. Above the entrance were twenty-five image-projection screens stretching nearly to the top of the Dome.

"With a United States Marine color guard and

an honorary color guard of famous Atlantans, please rise for our national anthem, performed by another famous Atlantan, John Mayer!"

Seventy-five thousand people placed their hands over their hearts. The announcer called out the names of the honorary color guard, including former NFL star Deion Sanders, comedian Jeff Foxworthy, and Ryan Seacrest, the host of *American Idol*. The guard stopped halfway down the Superstars' walkway; Mayer took his place in front of the marines and started to sing.

Shawn sneaked a glance at his mom and saw her wipe away a tear. He knew what she had to be thinking. If only Sanford could be here for this. If only.

The anthem ended. It was time for the main event: the wrestling!

WrestleMania opened with not one, but two Money in the Bank Ladder Matches, where eight Superstars competed at once. The winners needed to climb a ladder and retrieve a special briefcase. That briefcase gave them the right to challenge for the championship at a time and place of their own choosing.

In the first match, Randy Orton threw John Morrison off the top and snatched the briefcase from his hands to gain the victory. In the second,

Wade Barrett used the ladder to beat The Miz into submission and claim the briefcase.

Then Shawn Michaels was announced as the special guest referee for a Falls Count Anywhere Match between Jack Swagger and Triple H. Shawn was thrilled when his namesake stopped by the announcers' table to shake hands. In the contest, Swagger pinned Triple H right in front of the announcers' table.

A three-way tag-team contest followed between a huge-guys team of Mark Henry, Big Show, and The Great Khali and a high-flying team of R-Truth, Evan Bourne, and Daniel Bryan. No one gave the high-fliers much of a chance, but Bourne sent the crowd into a frenzy with an Air Bourne that brought down Big Show so hard that the impact tore the ring canvas.

The Divas championship was next. Michelle McCool and Natalya renewed their rivalry. Before the contest, Natalya took a microphone to give a shout-out to Jayden, whom she asked to stand and take a bow. The Dome responded with warm applause.

When the bell sounded, Natalya went to work on Michelle with a series of Michinoku drivers and snap suplexes.

As Natalya mounted a counterattack, two husky men with credentials around their necks and walkie-talkies in hand stopped at the announcers' table. They greeted Shawn warmly, introduced themselves as Zager and Evans—the taller of the two guys was Zager—and asked him to please come with them.

Zager explained, "Mr. McMahon wants to see you in the dressing room before the main event."

No way was Shawn going to keep Mr. McMahon waiting. So after an okay from the chaperones, he went back to tell his family where he was going.

"Can I come with?" Alex joked.

"No!" Peter responded. "Not unless I can come on this extrusion, too."

"*Excursion*, Peter. Excursion," Carla corrected him gently. "An extrusion is something that sticks out."

Zager came up behind Shawn. "Sorry, Peter. This is just for your brother."

The two WWE escorts led Shawn away to an elevator. They rode to the lowest level and then stepped out into a subbasement corridor lined with empty oil drums.

"Follow us," Evans instructed.

"You're sure this is the way to the locker room?" Shawn asked doubtfully.

Zager smiled confidently. "Back way in. In fact, here we are!"

They stopped at an unmarked door; Zager put out his hand for a shake before he opened it. "Have fun, SuperFan! This is going to be a night you'll never forget."

They shook, then Evans opened the door. Shawn hesitated. The room was dark.

"What's going—*oof!*"

Shawn felt himself shoved into the room; the door slammed shut behind him. As his eyes adjusted, he could see he was in some kind of storage room, lit by a single bulb.

"Hey! Hey! I'm in the wrong place! Hey!"

He heard Zager's low laugh on the other side. "See ya later, SuperFraud! Enjoy the show!"

"Wait a sec!" Shawn tried the door handle. It wouldn't budge. "Hey! Let me out!"

He tried the handle again. Nothing.

He was trapped.

CHAPTER TWENTY-FOUR

He pounded on the door. Kicked it. Banged against it with his body, all in a desperate attempt to get it to open. "Help! Somebody, open the door!"

No answer. Who would lock him in here? And why?

Shawn tried to stay calm. He found a switch and flipped it; the room was bathed in harsh fluorescent light, but it was better than the single bulb. He could see a small TV-DVD player combination.

He went to it and turned it on. It wasn't a regular television, but a monitor with a live feed from the ring.

What about that DVD player?

He pushed the Play button.

Spike Murcer's obnoxious face filled the screen.

"Hi, Shawn! SuperFan Spike here. I mean, not really Spike here. Spike upstairs. You here!" Spike cracked up. "Remember what Mr. McMahon said yesterday? How if the SuperFan couldn't do his duties for any reason, the runner-up would assume the job? Remember? Wait. Watch!"

As Shawn watched in horror, a clip from the

Ultimate SuperFan Challenge replaced Shawn on the monitor. It was Mr. McMahon:

We have two worthy competitors on hand. One will be the winner. The other, the runner-up, who will step into the role of SuperFan if the winner should be unable to continue for any reason.

"'For any reason,' Weenie Boy!" Spike repeated. "That means if you just happened to be locked in a basement when you're supposed to be carrying in the championship and I'm available, I'm the new SuperFan. Right, CM?"

Punk is in on this, too?

Shawn got his answer when Punk joined Spike on the screen. "It was so easy, Shawn. Hire a couple of big dudes. Fake their credentials. Call 'em Zager and Evans. Know who they were? A one-hit wonder rock duo from the sixties. Find the room. Set up this recording. It took about a half hour of fun!"

"But know what's going to be more fun?" Spike crowed. "Knowing you're watching. Or maybe we won't let you watch at all. Bye!"

The screen went black. Shawn turned the monitor off and on again. Nothing.

He sat on the floor and tried to contain his growing panic.

Feel it, he told himself. *Feel it till it goes away.*

It was the same technique he'd used with stage fright. Two minutes later, he wasn't frightened anymore. Just determined. He had two choices. He could stay down here and be found after the show. Or he could find a way to claim what is rightfully his.

He needed a way out. He checked the walls. Solid concrete. He looked down at the black floor. He looked up. It was a drop ceiling, like at home in Columbia . . .

Hey. Wasn't there space above a drop ceiling? He'd worked on the one in his room with his dad. Maybe that was his way out.

Carefully, he stood on the folding table and pushed at a ceiling tile. It came away easily; he let it drop to the floor.

Bingo.

There was auxiliary blue lighting that illuminated a suspended steel walkway.

Yes! Yes, yes, yes!

Shawn put both hands over the lip of the walkway. It was just like the pull-up bar in the doorway of his room. One good pull . . .

He was up. He was on the walkway. And he was running, hoping he wasn't too late.

CHAPTER TWENTY-FIVE

"Get out of this locker room!" Shawn ran up to Spike. "Now!"

"What are you doing here?" Spike exclaimed.

"What is going on?" Cena interrupted.

"Shawn, where have you been?" Rey demanded. "You were supposed to be here a half hour ago!"

Shawn pointed at Spike. "Ask him! Ask Punk! They planned it together."

"Planned what together?" Rey asked.

Face-to-face in the champions' dressing room with Spike, Shawn found himself angrier than he'd ever been in his life. The worst of it was that Spike didn't look sorry at all. He seemed to find the whole thing amusing.

"Go ahead, Spike," Shawn commanded. "Tell 'em what you did. Tell them!"

It was minutes after Shawn had escaped from the storage room. He'd run the catwalk until it ended at a steel ladder. That ladder deposited him outside another elevator, one supervised by a real WWE employee. When he explained what had happened the woman called everyone. A few moments later, a five-person WWE security group arrived to escort Shawn to the actual champions' locker room. There, Shawn found Spike with Cena's championship in his hands and Rey and Cena looking incredibly worried.

Rey took Shawn by the shoulders. "Shawn, talk to us."

Shawn talked. Three minutes was plenty of time to explain what Spike and CM Punk had done. When he was finished, a furious Rey turned to the guards, his voice dangerous. "Take this boy to his father. And then get them out of this arena before I throw them out. Spike? Give Shawn the championship. Now."

Spike hesitated for the briefest second.

"Now!" Rey thundered.

The championship made the quickest transition in the history of the WWE. Moments later, the security guys and Spike were gone.

"I am so sorry that happened," Cena told Shawn.

Shawn hardly heard him. He was mesmerized by the championship in his hands. The metalwork was beautiful, with Cena's name, the WWE logo, and a map of the world. How could a Superstar not long for it? A tap on his shoulder pulled him from his daydream. Cena and Rey were both standing over him. "Shawn?" Rey asked. "It's time."

The casket was at ringside. Sheamus had already made his entrance to thunderous boos. Lasers played on the Superstars' entrance as John Cena's theme music filled the Dome. The crowd revved up; stomping rattled the floorboards.

This is what WrestleMania is all about.

Rey was behind the Superstars' entrance with Shawn and Cena. For the last time, Shawn's mentor leaned down to talk one-on-one. "I brought another mask for you, amigo." Rey showed him a new wrestling mask. This one had the word SuperFan across the top. "But something tells me you won't be wanting it."

"Nope. I'm good." Shawn wanted people to see his face. He'd earned this.

"WWE Universe! Please welcome to the Georgia Dome, in his first official duty as the first-ever SuperFan . . . trained by Rey Mysterio, and carrying the WWE Championship for John Cena . . . from Columbia, Missouri, weighing in at ninety-nine pounds . . . Shawn Reynolds!"

"Go get 'em, Shawn," Rey exhorted. Shawn stepped into the arena. The fans went nuts, cheering for the skinny kid who a few months before didn't even like the WWE, the boy whose mother was a librarian and father was a soldier serving his country. Shawn thrust the championship skyward, taking in the love and giving back as much as he could.

"And from West Newbury, Massachusetts, weighing two hundred and forty pounds, the reigning WWE Champion, John Cena!"

Out came Cena. Shawn thought his eardrums might shatter as the crowd rocked the noise to another level. Meanwhile, in the ring, Sheamus glowered.

Suddenly, spotlights shifted to the top of the Dome. Shawn followed the beams. Unbelievable. Somebody was up there! Then whoever it was dropped down a rope like a commando, covering the distance to the floor in a few seconds.

Who was it?

CM Punk. He landed just five feet from Shawn and Cena.

"Well, well, well," Punk exclaimed into a mic. "If it isn't the so-called champ who's been ducking me for months! And the SuperFan champ-ette who couldn't fight his way off his mother's library cart!"

Cena found a microphone. "Go back to your hole, Punk."

"That coffin? I should be nailing you in it, Cena!"

"Hold on! Just hold on!"

Shawn watched as Sheamus stepped up to Punk and Cena. "You're suspended, Punk. You can't fight until Rey Mysterio says you can. This Casket Match is between Cena and me!"

CM Punk grinned. "I guess you're right, Sheamus. You definitely should live in a coffin!"

The crowd roared with laughter, as much as they didn't like CM Punk.

Sheamus crossed his massive arms. "Punk? Go back to your Straight Edge Society. And stay there!"

"I don't think so, Sheamus," Punk said evenly. "But I'm glad you reminded me about my suspension. I can't wrestle Cena officially. How about if I take him on unofficially?"

Without warning, CM Punk launched a flying dropkick that knocked Cena backward into the Superstars' entrance. As Cena tried to stand, a huge chunk snapped off the top of the structure and fell forty feet, landing on Cena's upper back. The champ doubled over in pain as boos and hissing shook the Dome.

It looked like Cena was hurt too badly to wrestle. Someone put a mic in his hands. "Thank . . . you . . . CM Punk. For ruining . . . the most important . . . event . . . of the year. WWE . . . Universe . . . says . . . thank you."

An impromptu chant of "Thank you, Punk!" started in the upper deck. Within moments, the whole Dome had picked it up. Punk took it as a compliment, conducting the crowd like an orchestra while Cena was helped backstage. Meanwhile, Sheamus stomped around like a madman. Punk had just ruined his title shot!

Suddenly, the crowd roared. The "Thank you, Punk!" chant gave way unexpectedly to Rey Mysterio's theme music. Shawn spun around. There was Rey, mic in hand, dressed for combat. "CM Punk, not only did you disappoint all these fans, but you disappointed me, too. I was looking forward to watching John Cena destroy you!"

Yeah! That's telling him. But don't challenge him, Rey. Your ankle!

Rey continued. "The WWE Universe deserves to see someone destroy you tonight! I think that someone is going to be me!"

"Rey, you're hurt, you can't fight!" Shawn shouted.

"I can and I will! I am sick of this guy!" Rey was infuriated.

Sheamus stepped between Rey and Punk. "Oh, no, you won't! This is my night to regain my crown. Take your feud someplace else!"

The crowd booed. Rey raised a hand for quiet. "You know what? Sheamus has a point. Here's my proposition: A two-on-one handicap match. Punk and Sheamus against me! And I want it to be an 'I Quit' Match!"

Sheamus blew up. "No! No! I want my title shot!"

Rey nodded. "Sheamus, thanks to Punk, you won't get a title match tonight. But if you two defeat me, the next time I'm champion—and I will be champion again—I will give you the very first shot at my title. That is my solemn promise. Do you gentlemen—and I use the term loosely—accept?"

Shawn looked at CM Punk, who was literally licking his lips at the chance to avenge his loss to Rey at last year's WrestleMania. The Celtic Warrior was less enthused, but understood that this was the best outcome he could ask for.

"I'm in," CM Punk declared.

"All right, Mysterio," Sheamus bellowed. "You've got your match!"

CHAPTER TWENTY-SIX

"This match will be a two-on-one handicap 'I Quit' Match. For Rey Mysterio to lose, he must tap out with the words *I quit*!"

"For the team of CM Punk and Sheamus to lose," the announcer continued, "the first member of that team can be pinned. The second member must tap out with the words *I quit*!"

Shawn stood ringside with Rey and shuddered. To battle both these Superstars at once? Nuts.

"I'm going to need your help," Rey told Shawn. "I need you to be my eyes and my ears. If someone is coming at me from behind, shout 'Blue Rey, Blue Rey!' If I've knocked someone out of the ring and they're coming back in, shout, 'Red Rey, Red Rey!' And if either of them picks up a weapon—a chair, a table, anything!—shout, 'Extreme Rey, Extreme Rey!' Got it?"

Shawn nodded. He had it.

Rey smiled grimly. "One more thing. Put on your new mask. For me."

Shawn did. The crowd saw it on the monitors and went absolutely wild.

"Okay, here we go," Rey declared.

He launched himself into the ring with a handspring as Sheamus and Punk climbed through the ropes. They'd clearly discussed strategy because they moved to opposite corners and started circling. Rey was forced to the center of the ring, where he whirled back and forth, trying to keep his opponents at bay. Shawn found himself constantly on the verge of shouting "Blue Rey!"

Then Sheamus and Punk struck.

By prearranged signal, the two Superstars rushed at Rey, who put up his hands to defend himself. Shawn expected a clothesline from the Celtic Warrior and an attack to Rey's midsection from Punk.

Instead, Sheamus unleashed a Brogue Kick—a flying bicycle kick designed to catch Rey on the chin. At the same time, CM Punk went for a spinning heel kick aimed at the same place. Executed well, both kicks were indefensible.

The kicks were executed exceptionally well. Shawn feared Rey would be knocked cold with a double concussion.

Somehow, Rey escaped destruction.

Shawn didn't know how he did it, but Rey leaped so high that the kicks passed underneath him. Then, still in the air, he grabbed Punk's leg and slung him toward the off-balance Sheamus.

Wham! Punk's right foot landed squarely on Sheamus's left temple. Sheamus crashed to the mat. Punk landed on top of him. Rey climbed quickly to the top of the ropes and launched a swan dive splash, landing on the Sheamus-Punk stack with sickening impact.

There was no need for him to cover. The Celtic Warrior was accidentally pinned by his own partner.

"One, two, three!" everyone chanted with the referee, the crowd joyous at the word *three*.

The match had become Rey versus CM Punk.

Rey ran to the corner where Shawn was standing below. "What'd you think of that?"

"Amazing!"

They shared a fist bump. "Same code as before," Rey reminded Shawn. "Because—"

Smash!

Oh no! I blew it, I blew it, I blew it!

It had been his job to keep an eye on CM Punk. But while he and Rey were congratulating themselves, Punk had gotten up, grabbed Rey, and whacked Rey's head into a turnbuckle.

Rey was helpless against the onslaught that followed. Punk did a Tilt-a-Whirl backbreaker. Then he heaved Rey to the far corner and drove his right shoulder into Rey's solar plexus. He followed with a series of knee strikes, then bounced twice off the ropes and smashed Rey with a springboard clothesline.

Rey crumpled. Punk stood over him, rubbing his chin as if trying to figure out how to get his final "I quit!"

"What do you think, Mysterio?" Punk shouted." I own you! You know what? Your family is still pitiful!"

The crowd booed louder than they'd booed all night. A year ago, it was Punk's ugly verbal attack on Rey's family that had turned their rivalry from ugly to thermonuclear. Now he was doing it again.

Punk made up his mind. He dropped to his knees and pulled Rey to a seated position. Then he grabbed Rey's right wrist and locked him in the dreaded Anaconda Vise. Though the move was illegal, either the ref didn't recognize it, or Punk was doing some variation that passed muster. In any case, Rey was a goner.

"Say 'I quit!' Say 'I quit!'" Punk screamed.

"Don't quit, Rey!" Shawn hollered at his mentor. All over the Dome, fans were shouting the same plea.

"Get to the ropes!" Shawn shouted. If Rey could somehow maneuver toward the ropes and hook even the tip of his toe, the referee would signal a break. "Rey! Get to the ropes!"

The Dome crowd picked up Shawn's encouragement. In a matter of seconds, a "619!" chant rocked the house. It seemed to give Rey strength.

"Six-one-nine!" Shawn joined the chorus.

Rey somehow got his left foot over the bottom rope.

"Break!" shouted the referee.

Punk broke. The Dome rocked with cheers.

The match wasn't over, though. Not even close.

Each Superstar had his chances. Rey used a frog splash on Punk, but Punk kicked out at two. Punk dropped Rey with a one-handed bulldog and a slingshot somersault senton; Rey was lucky to kick out at two-and-a-half. Rey actually knocked Punk out of the ring with a Dragonrana.

That was when Punk grabbed a steel chair.

"Extreme Rey! Extreme Rey!"

Shawn did his job perfectly. Rey leaped out of the ring and grabbed a chair in self-defense. For a moment, it was a standoff. Then Rey courageously threw his chair away and climbed back in the ring. Punk turned to the crowd, grinned, and faked tossing his chair away. No way was he giving up his weapon.

Just then, with Punk's back turned, Rey flung himself off the top rope and onto Punk with a moonsault that knocked his opponent to the concrete and sent the steel chair flying. Then Rey threw Punk back into the ring and unleashed a series of devastating, high-flying dropkicks.

After that came the 619 that put Punk flat on his back. Rey covered, and the crowd chanted, "One, two, three!"

The ref waved off the pin, since the rules called for an "I quit!"

Rey didn't hesitate. He wrapped up Punk in an inverted STF, locking his hands around Punk's head. Punk fought for the ropes the way Rey had minutes before, but Rey held him in center ring.

"Shawn! Shawn!"

Rey was calling to him. What for?

"Shawn! Get a mic! I want everyone to hear it!"

Shawn understood. He scrambled to the announcers' table and grabbed a microphone.

Then he ran up the steel stairs and into the ring, where Rey motioned to him to put the microphone by Punk's lips.

"Say it to Shawn, Punk. Say 'I quit!'" Rey demanded. He locked in the inverted STF even harder. Punk gasped in pain.

"I . . . I . . ."

"Say it!"

"I quit!" As if to underscore his words, Punk slammed his right hand against the canvas again and again, tapping out.

The match was over.

Rey sprang to his feet as the crowd roared. It roared louder when Shawn felt Rey grasp one of his hands and thrust it overhead as if they had been an actual tag team. The cheering was endless. Shawn thought it might be the greatest moment of his life. And it would have been, if only his dad were there.

CHAPTER TWENTY-SEVEN

As the cheers continued, Punk staggered away, defeated. Shawn turned toward the VIP section to wave to his mom, brother, and friends.

Huh. They weren't there. Was he looking in the right place? He sure was. But they were all gone. He didn't even see Taylor and his group.

Oh no, he thought. *Maybe Taylor had to be rushed to the hospital. Maybe everyone went with him and—*

"Members of the WWE Universe!" The public address system boomed one more time as the lights dimmed. "Please turn your attention to the Superstars' entrance to welcome a very special Superstar!"

Spotlights hit the entrance. Fireworks erupted. Patriotic scenes flashed on the screens. The Washington Monument. The Lincoln Memorial. Mount Rushmore. The Capitol. The White House.

It was a remarkable display. Whoever was coming in, he or she had to be big.

The fog machine pumped out red, white, and blue fog. Then the figure stepped out of the fog. A tall man in US Army fatigues.

Shawn's breath caught in his throat when he figured out who it was. "That's my dad! That's my dad! My dad is here!"

"Go to him!" Rey shouted.

As the announcer asked the WWE Universe to welcome Sergeant First Class Sanford Reynolds— father of SuperFan Shawn Reynolds, brought home from Afghanistan on a goodwill visit to see his son Shawn be a part of WrestleMania—Shawn ran to his dad.

No. He didn't run. He sprinted.

Moments later, Shawn was in his father's arms. He didn't even notice his friends and family step out from behind his dad. "When did you . . . when did you get here?" Shawn stammered.

His dad grinned as the cameras moved close enough to show everyone the scene as it unfolded. "Oh, yesterday."

"You got here yesterday?" Shawn was stunned.

"Yeah! Mom and I have known for a week that he was coming. We were privy!" Peter chortled. "And I used the word *privy* right, too!"

Shawn was shocked. "Why didn't you—"

"One good secret deserves another, right, Shawn?" His mother smiled slyly. "You kept it secret that you were thinking of entering SuperFan, right?"

Shawn protested. "Yeah, but that was different!"

Carla's grin grew wider. "Second reason? You read *Tom Sawyer*. Which means you know that sometimes you have to keep a secret in order to make a really, really big entrance!"

Shawn got it. His mom was talking about the scene where Tom and his friends had faked their own deaths in order to make a really, really big entrance at their own funeral service. Shawn thought it was the best scene in the book.

"I loved that scene," Sanford confided.

"You read *Tom Sawyer*?" Shawn raised his eyebrows. His mom was the big reader in the family.

"Shawn, you know what your mom says: Parents need to read the books that their kids are reading. I read *Tom Sawyer* in Afghanistan. Go ahead, quiz me," Sanford challenged, and seventy-five thousand people in the Dome roared with laughter.

"Where have you been staying?" Shawn asked.

"At the hotel," Sanford told him. "One floor below you. Go read my e-mails. I told you I was going on a special solo mission. *You* are the mission."

Sanford motioned for Rey to join him and Shawn, front and center. Carla stepped back; Rey came forward. The two men embraced to more cheers. Then Sanford held his hand up for quiet. The Dome hushed so quickly, you could have heard a butterfly land on a twig.

"I'm Sanford Reynolds," he announced. "My son is Shawn Reynolds. I think some of you might have heard of him!"

After a rolling wave of laughter, the Dome quieted again. "While I've been away serving our country, my son Shawn has grown from a boy to a young man. Rey Mysterio, I'm grateful for the guidance you've given him. Thank you, on behalf of my wife, Carla, and me."

More applause and cheering. Shawn looked up at his dad, his own eyes shining.

"We soldiers can't do it alone. For every one of us, there's a wife, a mother, a husband, a father, a sister, a brother, a son, or a daughter. Sometimes, one of each." Sanford looked meaningfully at his sons and wife. "When we're in the field, we can do our jobs because we know someone is minding the store back home. In my opinion? These people are as much heroes as we could ever be, and I want to recognize them right now. Can we bring the lights up in the arena, please?"

As the lights went to one hundred percent, Sanford took a few steps forward and asked his family to come forward with him.

"WWE Universe! If you're a military wife or a military mother—if your husband is in the service, or you're a mother with a child in the service, please rise and be recognized!" Sanford put both hands out as if to help these people to their feet. A thousand women around the arena stood. The cheers were overwhelming.

Sanford continued. "If you're a husband or father with a wife or children in the service, please rise!"

Hundreds more stood.

"If you're on active-duty military or have a parent on active duty, please rise!"

Hundreds more.

"If you've got a brother or a sister on active duty, please rise!"

And hundreds more.

"WWE Universe," Sanford asked. "Please recognize all these American heroes!"

Thousands were standing. The whole Dome was cheering. Shawn looked behind him. A number of Superstars had come out to witness his father's homecoming—Randy Orton, Evan Bourne, R-Truth, the members of the Hart Dynasty, including Natalya, even John Cena—and were applauding with everyone else.

Shawn had something to say. He asked for the microphone. Sanford gave it to him without hesitation.

Shawn took it and stepped forward, realizing that he was about to talk to seventy-five thousand people and wasn't feeling a bit of stage fright. Not a single bit.

"Thank you, WWE Universe. Thank you for WrestleMania, for SuperFan, for everything."

Impulsively, Shawn hugged his father. His mother joined the hug. So did his brother. Just beyond his dad, Shawn saw Rey looking on proudly.

"SuperFan. You." Rey held up a triumphant fist. "Booyaka!"

Shawn nodded.

That's right. SuperFan. Me. Now and forever.

THE END